ONE EPIC RING

ONE EPIC RING

THE UNBELIEVABLE MR. BROWNSTONE™ BOOK FOURTEEN

MICHAEL ANDERLE

LMBPN Publishing
PMB 196, 2540 South Maryland Pkwy
Las Vegas, NV 89109

First US edition, December 2018
Version 1.04, January 2021

THE ONE EPIC RING TEAM

Special Thanks
to Mike Ross
for BBQ Consulting
Jessie Rae's BBQ - Las Vegas, NV

Thanks to the JIT Readers

Micky Cocker
Misty Roa
Angel LaVey
John Ashmore
Mary Morris
Kelly O'Donnell
Peter Manis
Keith Verret
Nicole Emens
James Caplan
Paul Westman

If I've missed anyone, please let me know!

Editor
Lynne Stiegler

*To Family, Friends and
Those Who Love
to Read.
May We All Enjoy Grace
to Live the Life We Are
Called.*

CHAPTER ONE

This shit is even better the third time.

James swallowed his last bite of pulled pork and bread, taking a moment to let the flavors of the sauce from his sandwich play across his tongue. Jessie Rae's had never disappointed him in the past, and today's lunch was no different.

I need to be studying this; always paying attention to all the flavors and textures. If I ever want to surpass Jessie Rae's, I'm gonna have to understand Mike's cooking. Sorry, Mike, but someday I'll take you down.

James wasn't sure if that was even possible, but no point in picking an unworthy adversary to test his skills against.

"I don't know if I can finish mine," Trey commented from across the table. "But *damn*, is that one of the best pork sandwiches I've ever had!" He leaned forward. "Don't tell Nana, but this is way better than hers. She'd beat my ass for blasphemy and disrespect."

James nodded. "I won't tell her. I need you alive to work bounties."

Maria smirked. "That is a lot of Brownstone to fit in your mouth. I don't know if Tyler would approve."

James glanced at the two and grunted. "Even if it's the Brownstone Sandwich, it's technically a Brownstone *Agency* sandwich. I think it's pretty damned good, myself. Worth waiting a few months for Mike to figure it out, not that I didn't think he'd pull it off."

The owner of Jessie Rae's had promised James and Trey a new sandwich after they'd returned his stolen memorabilia and awards but had quickly found himself conflicted about how to best express their bravery in sandwich form. What meat and cut best spoke to justice? What sauce best highlighted a man's strength of will? What bread screamed "badass?"

James didn't mind the wait. That was the kind of drama he could handle. Even though he'd taken down a few level-four bounties in the last couple of months, things had been mostly quiet since Alison had returned to school after Christmas break.

After the Wendigo adventure in Canada, James had decided to stay home for Christmas. He didn't want some nanoform ruining Alison's Christmas vacation by trying to take him out. She worried about him even more than he worried about her.

Christmas vacation had been a fun time, not a violent one. No weird energy monsters attacking them. No one trying to blow up his house. No mystery Drow stepping through a portal and challenging him to single combat. Just a relaxing time at home, a family and their dog.

That alien bitch is still out there, but at least she isn't fucking with Jessie Rae's. That makes her smarter than Demetrius. I hope those nanites were real damned expensive. Maybe she gave up after I beat her nanite shit down.

He didn't believe that, but hope never harmed a man, especially when his stomach was filled with delicious meat. He also liked the idea of building up an interplanetary reputation.

How many aliens will I have to beat down before everyone in the fucking galaxy knows not to mess with me?

Maria smiled. "It's nice that Mike did this after you guys tracked down that thief, and it's cool having an agency sandwich." She frowned at hers. She'd given up on the mammoth edible monument to the glories of sauced pork. "But does it really take that long to figure out a barbeque sandwich? It's barbeque, not brain surgery."

James grunted. "Yeah, brain surgery's easier. Not like there are a bunch of different regional brain surgery styles."

Trey laughed. "North Carolina brain surgery, Kansas City brain surgery, Texas brain surgery."

James chuckled and shook his head. "It'll be years before I'll be able to attempt the kind of shit Mike is pulling off in this sandwich. You have to balance not just the meat and sauce, but also how they play off the bread. There are so many different things you have to take into account. It's complicated as shit, but the good kind of complicated."

Trey nodded his agreement, his face solemn. "You should join PFW, Maria. Once you start cooking with us, you'll understand. I thought I liked barbeque before, but once I was on the team, I started to love and *understand* barbeque. I know so much shit now that I didn't know about before. I thought I was a barbeque man, but I was just a barbeque boy waiting to become a man."

"First of all," Maria replied with a laugh, "I don't want to be a boy *or* a man. Second, you make it sound like a cult or a bunch of junkies. I think I should stay well clear of it."

Trey shot her a grin. "Hey, it ain't so bad. Barbeque is better than drugs. Might be cheaper to be an addict, though."

They both laughed.

James stared at the menu on the wall, wondering if he should go for another sandwich or some ribs, especially since he hadn't been making it up to Vegas as much as he wanted lately. He scratched his chin as he considered the possibilities.

Trey's phone buzzed, and he pulled it out of his pocket. He stared down at it for a moment as he read the message. "Huh. Didn't expect that. Don't know whether to be annoyed or surprised."

James continued to stare at the menu, weighing his choices versus the annoyance he might inflict on Trey and Maria by making them stay since they'd all driven there in his truck.

"What's up?" Maria asked, far less entranced by barbeque.

Trey looked her way. "Remember Marty Calabrese?"

She eyed his phone. "Oh, did that cockroach finally scuttle out from under someone's refrigerator? Anywhere close? Something about his smug face makes me want to bring him in that much more."

"He's damn close. He's in Vegas." Trey grinned. "I mean, he's all but begging us to find him and bring him in. Probably sitting in his house being all, 'I think Trey and Maria are bitches. They can't get me.'"

Curiosity defeated barbeque, if only for a moment, and James looked at the other bounty hunters. "Who the fuck is Marty Calabrese?"

"Makes sense you don't know about him offhand." Trey shrugged. "He's a level three. Do you even check level threes anymore?"

James shook his head. "That's what I've got the agency for. I concentrate on the big fish that come through and let you guys handle everything else." He shrugged. "Since Zoe gave you those gloves, there's even less reason for me to get involved. I'm trying to take it easy. Shay suggested I try it out for a while." He grunted.

Trey laughed. "Beating down level fours is easy?"

"Only taken down a few lately." James shrugged. "I'd go after a level five, but none of those fuckers have come to LA lately."

"Sure, big man, sure. Anyway, that bitch Calabrese is a former Mafia enforcer." Trey snorted. "He was supposed to be in Witness Protection in Wichita, but crime's too fun for the motherfucker to give it up. He started a dust ring and killed a guy during a bad deal. Some people were saying back in December that he was coming to Vegas to settle some scores, so we've been looking around for the piece of shit but haven't been able to find him."

"And?" James had almost settled on ordering another Brownstone Sandwich before his mind flipped back to ribs.

"And my boy who sent me the message here says he's got a line on Marty at this huge-ass rental house, but he also says our boy Marty's hired a big new crew. He's about to make some noise. Settle some scores." Trey shrugged. "I thought we was coming just for the sandwich, and we don't have another crew coming in until tomorrow since things have been light on the ground the last few days. Victoria's out of town, too. Maybe we should wait. Taking Calabrese on when he's got a whole crew with him might be annoying as fuck."

Maria frowned. "If your informant has a line on him, Calabrese might find out and run. The dirt bag's done a good job of hiding so far. If we don't make a move on him now, he might not be there tomorrow. He could end up in rural Idaho for months. You want to look for him there?"

"Me and the country don't agree," Trey mumbled, fluffing his lapels. "This is city style. Too much dust and shit will ruin my fine threads." He looked at James. "Then again, we don't need a crew if we've got the big man. That's if you want to come and play with us just for a level three and his buddies."

James shrugged. "I've got nothing better to do." He nodded at his empty plate. "I'm done with my sandwich anyway."

"You sure you're not gonna order another one, big man? That's your third." Trey chuckled. "Don't want you to have to go out into the world starving to death. Sad, sad end for the Granite Ghost."

"I was actually thinking about ribs, but I can order those to go." James wiped his hands with a napkin. "Let me do that, then we'll go have a chat with Calabrese and his friends. This shit might be fun."

James parked his black F-350 across the street from the huge two-story house. A tall white fence surrounded the property, but the front gate stood open. Nothing about the well-maintained lawn gave any hint that a criminal gang might be living inside.

If he isn't in there, I don't want to go shooting up the place and annoying the local cops for no good reason.

"How do we want to do this?" Trey asked, nodding toward the brick walkway leading to the front porch. He slipped on his enchanted gloves and patted his chest to check his bulletproof vest. "Just have James kick in the door and start beating ass? Give them a chance to surrender?"

Even if they hadn't come fully equipped, James always kept some supplies in the back of his truck in case he and Shay needed to kick a little ass. Taking down a mobster and his guards didn't warrant much more than guns, stun rods and bulletproof vests, especially given that James would go in with his amulet and Trey his gloves.

Maria shook her head as she clipped a stun rod to her belt. "We need to make sure Calabrese doesn't run. If he escapes, it doesn't matter how many random idiots we take down. They might not have bounties on them, and he's the damned mastermind anyway. He's the one running the dust rings."

She narrowed her eyes. Maria had proven to be an asset to the agency, but sometimes James forgot she'd spent decades as a cop. Priorities were hard to reset.

James grunted. "Maybe you two should take the back,

and I'll knock on the front door. If they've got any surprise shit, I can take it better. Just because it's supposed to be a level three doesn't mean we won't find He Who Hunt's cousin in there."

"Sounds like a good plan, big man." Trey nodded. "Oh, forgot to tell you earlier—this shit ain't dead or alive, at least not for Calabrese. Gonna need you to dial it down to badass."

James frowned. "Do we know about bounties on the other guys?"

Trey shook his head and shrugged. "Don't know who else he's got in there, so I can't say."

James reached into the open suitcase in the back seat and grabbed a few throwing knives. "Then the other assholes should stay out of the way if they don't want to die."

"Probably, but you still need to control yourself," Maria replied. She chuckled and opened the door. "Just remember, explosions are indiscriminate. We need Calabrese mostly breathing when we deliver him to the Vegas PD."

James nodded. "You showed me his picture. I know what he looks like and I won't kill anyone who looks like him." He shrugged. "You two make your way around back. I'll hit the front in a minute."

Trey and Maria stepped out of the truck and ran down the side fence. Stealth wasn't that important. Even if the pair were spotted, the men inside would soon have someone large, angry, and tattooed to draw their attention.

Once the other bounty hunters had moved out of sight, James took a deep breath and reached under his shirt to remove the spacer separating his amulet from his body. He gritted his teeth as the amulet extended its tendrils into his body, burning pain accompanying their spread.

Initiation, Whispy sent.

Don't really need you for this shit, but Alison whined at me again about being careful, James thought. *So, congrats, time to go all pro level on these junior varsity assholes.*

Constant use improves tactical capability and adaptation potential. Engage and kill enemies. Achieve primary directive.

These guys aren't going to feed you today. Just some guns, maybe a knife or two.

The amulet projected a faint undercurrent of annoyance. *Kill stronger enemies for maximum adaptation.*

Could be worse, James responded. *I could not use you at all.*

He snorted and crossed the street. The last thing he needed was a prima donna amulet. He'd spent most of his adulthood using Whispy Doom as nothing more than glorified armor, not realizing its true potential. Now that another alien was hunting him, Whispy might be the only thing that would keep him from getting his ass kicked. The damned thing needed to work when he wanted it to work and without a lot of attitude. It was almost like the fucking symbiont thought *he* should be the one calling the shots.

The bounty hunter walked up the path to the door, his boots clopping on the brick. Several Andercarr delivery boxes were piled in front of the door. He knew the reason for the open gate now, although it increased the chance no one was at home.

"Did the fucker run?" James murmured. "Can't settle scores if you're already running, Calabrese. Don't be such a pussy."

James stopped in front of the door and rang the doorbell. The lack of response led him to knock hard on the door.

"Damn it," he muttered. "Don't have all fucking day. If he wasn't even going to be here, I should have just stayed at Jessie Rae's and had another sandwich before I ordered the ribs. Calabrese better be here if he doesn't want to really piss me off."

James pounded on the door again, not breaking it down only because he couldn't be certain that Trey's informant hadn't sent them to some random innocent person's house. He'd promised Mack and Maria he'd try to cut down on unnecessary property destruction. It'd help keep his insurance rates down, too.

The door swung open to reveal a man who had several inches on James. The thug's chest and arms strained his ill-fitting suit, and the thick muscles of his neck forced James to take an extra second to distinguish the man's head from his body.

The neckless wonder looked James up and down before glancing at the boxes, a frown on his face. "The fucking delivery company knows we don't need to sign. We're fucking tired of telling them that, so get the fuck out of here, dumbass. It's not like you work for tips." He slammed the door.

James grunted and rapped on the door again.

The thug threw the door open and stepped onto the porch. He pulled the door closed behind him. "You really want to get hurt, don't you, delivery boy? You think you're big shit because you've got a few tats? Maybe I should knock some fucking sense into you like I did the tatted-up loser I fucked up during my last spin in the joint."

MICHAEL ANDERLE

10

"I'm not with the fucking delivery company, and you're starting to piss me off." James grunted. "Take a look, dumb-ass. Do I look like I'm wearing a fucking Andercarr uniform?"

Give me a reason, asshole. You've already pissed me off.

The other man frowned, staring at James for a moment. His eyes narrowed as if the possibility of James not being a delivery man had never occurred to him. "Then who the fuck are you? Is this some buy-eBook-subscriptions-because-I'm-fresh-out-of-prison shit? I'm not buying your fucking subscription. Go get a job, leech."

"I have a job," James rumbled.

The other man sneered. "What job is that?"

"Bounty hunter."

The neckless wonder laughed. "Oh, really?"

"Yeah, I'm James Brownstone," the bounty hunter growled. "I'm here for Marty Calabrese. I don't know who the fuck you are or if you have a bounty on you, so stay the fuck out of my way if you want to live."

The thug snorted. "That supposed to scare me? Fucking a bunch of reporters or something to convince 'em to run stories about you don't impress me. This ain't California crystal-shit LA, Brownstone. This is Vegas, and we don't play. Get the fuck out of here before I put a bullet in your ass."

He opened the door, entered, and slammed it shut, snickering all the while.

James let out another low growl. "Fine. We'll do this the hard way then, fucker. I'm gonna do what that relationship podcast said and actualize my words into reality."

Yes, Whispy hissed in his mind. *Hatred. Anger.*

Nah. This is just me being fucking annoyed.

James had been on the fence about bothering with a level three, but he obviously hadn't been working enough bounties in Vegas. He needed to make a point so that the next time he showed up at an asshole's door in Vegas, they'd understand why it hurt less to do what he said.

"Guess you always got to keep feeding fame if you want your rep to stay." James cracked his knuckles and kicked the door off its hinges. "My fucking public awaits."

CHAPTER TWO

The door flew several yards before crashing to the floor with an echoing *thump*. The neckless wonder from before stood a few feet to the side, staring at the door as if he'd just witnessed a miracle. A half-dozen other men, most in tracksuits but a few in tank tops, jeans, and gold chains shot up from the couch and chairs filling the room, surprise on their faces.

They gathered their wits and drew their weapons, turning their angry eyes on James.

He didn't bother to pull his gun. Instead, he swept the room with a glare. There was no way any of these idiots could hope to do much more than scratch him. "Where the fuck is Marty Calabrese? I'm not here for you, so tell me where he is and fuck off if you want to keep breathing."

The door thug raised his gun. "Fuck you, Brownstone. You ain't nothing."

He pulled the trigger. The bullet struck James and bounced off with barely a sting. It wasn't even worth a grunt.

The thug blinked and backed up. He gritted his teeth.

Minimum adaptation potential, Whispy reported. *Kill enemies.*

James chuckled. The amulet never changed his general advice. Strong enemies, weak enemies—it didn't matter. Kill them and move on. There was a certain comfort in that kind of consistency.

Killing gangsters who had attacked him didn't bother James, but he did want to avoid unnecessary paperwork with the police.

These fuckers are going to add several hours to my trip, aren't they?

James stared at the man. "There are two ways this can go down, fucker. I can just go through you all until I find Calabrese, or you can—"

The man fired again. The bullet bounced off James' head, leaving a small scratch.

"What the fuck?" the neckless thug exclaimed. "Help me kill this asshole, guys."

Everyone opened fire now, bullet after bullet striking James and bouncing off even as they perforated his clothes. He grunted a few times, but the impacts were more distracting than painful.

Knew I should have put another spare shirt and pants in the damned truck. Time to end this shit. They had their chance.

James bellowed and charged the neckless wonder. The man backed away, his lip quivering as he ejected his magazine and reloaded. A powerful backhand from James sent him flying over a chair. The thug landed on the floor, blood dripping from his split lip.

The other men continued firing, the sound not

drowning out the thud of footsteps coming down the stairs.

"This shit's gonna take too long," James muttered. "Fuck it. Maybe the Vegas PD will let me do the paperwork later."

He nailed several men in the throat or head with throwing knives. Whether from fear or bravery, the rest didn't break and run, so he yanked out his .45 and put rounds into the survivors.

Their guns fell silent, and the few still alive moaned on the floor.

Reinforcements pelted the corner, shotguns and assault rifles in hand. They didn't wait to take in the situation before firing at James.

This combined volley stung, but the pain faded within seconds, and the few scratches and cuts started sealing. Advanced mode might be required for James' best weapons and full defense, but the amulet's regeneration had improved even with only basic bonding.

A wave of annoyance flashed from the amulet. *Minimum adaptation potential. Kill enemies. Seek stronger enemies for maximum adaptation potential.*

James chuckled. *Sometimes you just need to blow off some steam. Don't worry. Maybe we'll get lucky and run into some thug with nanites.*

His magazine was empty, so he tossed the weapon into his left hand and grabbed a nearby coffee table. He spun and hurled the heavy cherrywood table. The thugs' bullets ripped into the table and blew several holes in the projectile before it shattered on two riflemen. They fell back, yowling in pain.

The makeshift formation scattered, giving James

precious seconds to reload. By the time his enemy rallied, he had rushed forward and was firing again. The men fell one by one, their screams echoing through the house.

James stomped over to the bodies, frowning as he ejected his empty magazine and reloaded again. At this rate, he was going to run out of ammo and need to use the dead thugs' guns.

A steep staircase lay at the end of a hallway around the corner, changing angles ninety degrees halfway up. No one was up there.

"Where the fuck is Calabrese?" James roared. "Don't make me come and find you, asshole. I'm already pissed about all the extra reports I'm gonna have to fill out about your fucking men."

Trey's hands twitched as gunfire sounded inside. "Maybe we should go in. He might need help."

Damn. I should just have gone in with the big man. Two people watching the back? What's up with that bullshit?

Maria shook her head and flattened herself against the wall next to the door, a stun rod ready. "No, the point is to get Calabrese. No way Brownstone is getting seriously hurt by guns. We've both seen what it takes to make that guy bleed. He took on King Pyro in a fist fight, and that guy could melt steel with his hands."

"But I'm bored as shit," Trey complained. "James is having all the fun." He stared longingly at his gloves. "These boys are itching for me to pound a face or two. Zoe ain't said so, but maybe they lose their power if they don't meet a quota, you know?"

Maria smirked. "Don't worry, some of those losers will be coming this way soon enough. I hear footsteps. Maybe we'll even get lucky and it'll be Calabrese. Feel free to punch him." She shook a finger at him. "But remember, we need the asshole alive."

"I will, and I appreciate your generosity." Trey grinned and pushed his knuckles together.

Maria held up her left hand and narrowed her eyes. Trey crouched, ready to pounce on whoever or whatever came through the door.

The door flew open, and a sad, pathetic man in nothing but a sweat-stained undershirt and boxer shorts emerged at the forefront of a column of fleeing thugs, their faces etched with terror. They were so intent on fleeing that none of them bothered to look to the side.

Maria let several go past before she stunned the first man. Trey launched himself into the group and threw several quick punches. Each powerful blow sent a man crashing to the ground in pain.

One thug managed to get his gun out before Trey slammed a fist into his stomach. The man flew back into the house, knocking several other fleeing criminals down. A collective groan rose from the stunned men.

"This shit's like bowling," Trey announced.

Maria and Trey rushed inside past the downed men to stun or knock out the rest while most of the thugs were still fumbling for their weapons. The fear only built on their faces as they realized they'd fled from a monster only to run into his friends.

"It's like they're running from a fucking dragon. Thought they were all badasses? Hope Calabrese didn't pay too much for these bitches." Trey laughed. "Might have some bounties off these fuckers, though." Trey grabbed some zip-ties. "Let's just tie them together in pairs. We should have enough for that. I only have a couple of pairs of cuffs."

A loud, thumping rattle shook the building, and the roar of a heavy machine gun echoed from upstairs.

"That's a big gun," Maria yelled. She jammed her stun rod into her pocket.

Trey shrugged as he shoved two groaning men together and bound their hands. "James is starting some shit with someone a little tougher than these rats fleeing the sinking ship. Ain't no thing."

Maria knelt to zip-tie another pair of men. "I hope he remembers we have to take this guy alive to get any money."

The thug's chain gun shredded the banister as James crested the stairs. The bullets slammed into him and fell to the floor, crumpled. Thin trails of blood leaked from cuts on his body, and pain radiated from his ribs. The stream of bullets forced him back, teeth gritted, then he leapt to the top of the stairs and fired three quick shots into the chest of the gunner.

The criminal fell back, his finger still on the trigger for a few seconds. The bullets ripped through the roof, and dust, wood, and insulation showered down. A few sparks shot from exposed wires in the ceiling.

James grunted. Blood covered the front of his chest, but his wounds were already beginning to heal, the pain dulling. The adventure against Calabrese and his men was proving enlightening.

Used to be even something like that would still be a decent hit, even with you on, Whispy. I've been shot tons of times, but it's that much better now?

Improved baseline defensive capabilities associated with achievement of advanced transformation and permanent interface body modification, Whispy responded.

James snorted. He wasn't sure if that meant the amulet had been holding back on him all these years because he didn't understand the whispers or if there was a more fundamental change in how Whispy's defenses worked. Either way, he was satisfied with the results.

So if I play your game and get pissed, James thought, *you have an easier time improving my abilities?*

High levels of power necessary for long-term and efficient adaptation and modification of host.

James grunted. Whatever kept him breathing was fine by him.

A door squeaked open, and a man in a belted blue robe walked out, gun in one hand, oblong silver grenade in the other.

James looked the man over for a moment and chuckled. Sometimes people on the run tried to change their appearance because that split second of confusion could help them escape, but Marty Calabrese still had the exact same damned haircut as in his mugshots and bounty records.

"You really like your style, huh, Calabrese?" James rumbled.

"James Brownstone? Shit. Just my damned luck." The man stared at him, wild-eyed. "Fuck. Why aren't you dead?" He shook his head. "You're shredded. They must have hit you a hundred times."

"Yeah, that sounds about right." James nodded at the dead machine-gunner. "He might have hit me that many times himself. It kind of stung. Made me even more pissed." He shrugged.

Calabrese narrowed his eyes. "Your chest is all fucked up, though. It's like something got jammed in there. What the fuck is up with that?"

James glanced down. The annihilation of his shirt exposed the bonded amulet. He chuckled and patted the alien artifact. Calabrese's guess wasn't far from the truth.

"Marty Calabrese," James rumbled. "You're coming with me. You have a little appointment with the Vegas police." He pointed at the dead gunner. "I've taken out all your guys, or they've run their asses away because they knew they didn't stand a fucking chance. Your crew is gone, so don't be a dumbass."

Calabrese shook his head. "Screw them and screw you, Brownstone." He held up the grenade. "Maybe you've got some bulletproof artifact shit, but you can't survive this nice little toy I got from a friend of mine. He got it from the CIA or some shit like that. Don't know fuck-all about how it works, but it blows up real good, he says. Can melt a car. Been waiting to try it, so you should be honored. Great James Brownstone's gonna die by my ultimate weapon, not some bitch-ass gun."

James shrugged. "A fancy grenade won't save your ass. You come with me, you don't die. If you try to fight me, you might. I guarantee you're gonna get hurt. Easy fucking choice, from where I stand."

Calabrese scoffed. "I go back into the system, I'll be dead in three months anyway. This way I take the famous James Brownstone with me and become a legend."

James growled. "Not my fault you're too much of a fucking dumbass to not cause trouble in Witness Protection, so get rid of the grenade and make this shit easy or not—I don't give a fuck. Just make it quick."

The mobster raised the grenade. "Back right the fuck off now, Brownstone, or you get to see how your tax dollars are spent up close."

James shrugged. "You're not escaping, asshole. It's just a matter of how much pain you want to feel first."

Calabrese glared at him and hurled the grenade. "Fuck you." He leapt into the bedroom and closed the door.

Estimated adaptation potential minor, Whispy reported.

James jumped over the railing as a blue-white explosion enveloped him. The force of the blast accelerated him toward the ground. He smashed into the hardwood planks on the first floor, the wood splintering and cracking.

The explosion had done some of its work, turning his clothes into burned scraps and his gun and phone into molten goo. Burns covered his body, and the cool breeze of the air conditioning stung. Whatever the hell Calabrese had thrown at him, it was far from a standard-issue fragmentation grenade.

Huh. Really must have been some fancy CIA crap. I thought he was just talking shit.

Moderate adaptation to attack forces, Whispy sent. *Moderate damage. Regeneration in progress. Full tactical restoration not immediate. Kill enemy.*

Mild satisfaction flowed from the amulet.

James grunted. Nothing like a masochistic defensive artifact.

Now the fucker's gone and made me mad.

He stood, frowning at the fused mass on the floor that used to be his phone. His pain would go away, but he could never recover wasted time. He had everything backed up in the cloud, but that still meant he was going to have to waste time going to a damned store to buy a new phone and re-download everything.

And I had that shit set up just the way I like it.

"Damn," Trey announced from behind him. "You all right?"

"He tried to blow me up," James rumbled. "I survived, and now I'm really fucking pissed."

Maria chuckled. "Yeah, I can see that." She shook her head.

Trey circled James with a frown and sucked in a breath through his teeth. "You're all burned, big man. Damn, that shit looks like it hurts like a motherfucker."

"I've had worse." James frowned and looked around for his healing potion. The shattered remnants of the bottle were scattered near the cooling mass of metal that used to be his .45. "Fuck, I lost my potion when I hit the ground. That was my favorite .45, too." He grunted. "Got others back at home, but still, fuck that asshole." He winced.

Maria cleared her throat. "Not that I'm eager to tell Shay about this, because she'll probably slit my throat, but you're also naked, Brownstone. Might want to do something about that."

He grunted. "I'll borrow some clothes from one of the dead guys. Fucking CIA grenade."

"No way in hell," shouted Calabrese, standing by what remained of the second-floor railing.

Half of it had been burned away. Massive scorch marks covered the walls, floor, and ceiling all the way to the top of the stairs. Smoke floated up from smoldering and charred wood.

He stared down at Brownstone, his mouth agape. After a few seconds, he crossed himself and shook his head.

James glared up at the man, extra annoyed that the bastard was asking for help from Above when he was a criminal piece of shit.

"You just made my day very fucking annoying, Calabrese," James shouted. "That was one of my favorite guns. Get the fuck down here before I break every damn bone in your body. The bounty says alive, but it doesn't say shit about uninjured. You should feel lucky I don't fucking kill you for making my life more complicated."

The mobster swallowed and tossed his gun to the floor. He hurried to the stairs, bounding down two at a time while Maria and Trey pointed their weapons at him. Calabrese hurried over to Brownstone, collapsed to his knees, and spun around, his hands on his head, surrendering.

"Fuck, fuck, fuck," the mobster shouted. "I fucking threw some super-grenade at you and you're not dead. How the fuck does that happen? That shit would have fried AET in full armor."

"I'm not fucking AET." James chuckled.

Maria snickered and rolled her eyes. "That's for sure."

Trey laughed. "You dumbass motherfucker, you think the big man taking on all those badasses before was just a dream or something?"

The other man shook his head. "I don't care anymore. Take me to the police. I give up."

"What's the matter?" Trey taunted. "Not a big shot now? Thought you came back to Vegas to settle some scores?"

Calabrese shook his head. "I'd take on every hitman in the country before I take on Brownstone again after what I just saw."

James snorted. "About fucking time you got it, dumbass." He borrowed a zip tie from Trey and secured the prisoner. "You move without my say-so and I'll break something."

The bounty nodded quickly.

"You check the survivors for bounties," James rumbled. "I'm gonna put some fucking clothes on."

He looked around in search of an alternate outfit. There was too much blood on all the men he'd shot, not to mention the holes from the bullets. It was time to raid the closets.

CHAPTER THREE

Aiyn sighed as she stared out at the ocean. Her status reports flowed across her ocular implants, bringing her nothing but continuing disappointment. She'd hoped for something positive, but the last couple of months had trained her to expect the message before her now.

Interunit nanite bonding past sustainable levels. Batch bonding failure beyond critical mass. Nanite regeneration cycle reinitiated.

She took small comfort in the fact that the nanite regeneration was only slowed, not halted, but a delay meant her enemy had time to grow stronger while her best weapon remained unavailable. Given the time that had passed, she should have already been close to replenishing her supply, but it would be months before she had a workable supply, let alone enough to take on Brownstone again directly.

Maybe if I adjust the parameters and field strengths again, it'll improve speeds? There has to be something I can do. If only I could ask for engineering support.

Aiyn took a deep breath and slowly let it out, trying to fight off the frustration screaming to spill out. She'd been so *close* in Canada, without leaving any real evidence. Once she'd handed Brownstone's corpse over to the Alliance, any punishment she received would have been minor and the Earth would have been safe.

But she'd failed. Completely and utterly failed.

The mighty Forerunner had been wounded, not killed, and going after him again without a nanoform would be suicide. She didn't mind dying, but only if she took him with her.

Aiyn dropped into her chair and rubbed the bridge of her nose, hoping to ease the slight ache in her forehead. Nanoforms were always temperamental, but she'd never expected to have so much trouble replenishing her supply.

Her reports to the Alliance had conveniently left out her attempt on Brownstone's life, and asking for direct resupply would lead to the discovery of what she'd done. Whatever hope she might have had of the Alliance solving the problem had long since vanished.

Whether it was bureaucracy, arrogance, or simple cowardice preventing them from heeding her warning she couldn't be sure, but it didn't change the fact that she was one of the few beings on Earth or Oriceran who stood a chance of staving off their destruction.

Aiyn shook her head. She couldn't be taken from Earth until she completed her task. It was time for lateral thinking.

Most of her scenarios that would guarantee a victory over Brownstone involved too much collateral damage.

She would not sink to the level of the Vax and kill innocent people. She was a Shepherd.

I will protect them, even if I die without them ever knowing I existed.

But I failed to convince Shay Carson to turn on him. Now he's on defense, and he has an advantage because he probably knows that an advanced race is hunting him

I've made mistakes, but I still have a chance. No new Vax have arrived. That has to mean something. He isn't ready yet, which means he feels he's vulnerable. I must exploit that window of vulnerability.

That woman has to be the key, but how can I manipulate her? Even if she's serving him, she's close to him in a way we've never seen before. That has to be useful in some way.

Probing further into Shay's background didn't turn up much Aiyn didn't already know. She'd been a professional killer and left that life behind to become a tomb raider after faking her own death. The cover-up of her past had been clever and thorough, but enough strands had remained for the determined Shepherd to uncover the truth.

Shay's choice of clients and interaction with some of her less violent tomb raider competitors suggested she was no longer the ruthless killer she'd once been. There were more than a few hints of a conscience, which wasn't consistent with serving a vicious alien who would bring on an invasion and genocide.

Could I turn her if I explained the whole truth? Even if she knows that he's an alien, I doubt he told her that he plans to bring his people here to lay waste to the Earth.

That afraid of magic, are you, Vax? The Oricerans have

forced you to crawl around and hide. So proud, but brought so low. But you can't maintain that, can you? It goes against your nature, and it's just a matter of time now, isn't it, before you destroy and murder like you always do?

Aiyn tapped her AllBand a few times to check the status of some of her dark web searches. The presence of magic presented the same disadvantage to her technology as it did the Vax's, but that meant it also gave her opportunity not available anywhere else she might encounter the enemy.

There has to be something I can use. Something even better than the nanites.

Her breath caught as results filtered in.

"That could work," she murmured, looking at the search results. "I just need to time this correctly." Aiyn smiled. "This will be satisfying in ways you can't begin to imagine, Brownstone."

Trey waved at James from his front porch. It was good to be back in LA.

The team had had to stay overnight in the Vegas Brownstone loft. By the time they'd dropped Calabrese off and made it through the paperwork associated with the non-bounty fatalities, it had been too damned late for a road trip.

Several of Calabrese's crew had turned out to have their own bounties, but James' enthusiasm for killing people had reduced the rewards they'd received since none of the men's bounties were dead or alive. Despite that, due to his sheer volume and Maria and Trey capturing more than a few level twos in the back of the house, the whole day had ended up profitable enough.

The roads were nice and clear early the next morning, so the bounty hunters made good time returning to LA.

James looked at Maria in the passenger seat. "Dropping you off at your place or Tyler's?"

Neither was all that close, but it wasn't like he had anything all that important to do that morning other than go get a new phone.

Maria smiled. "My place for now. Tyler's already at the Black Sun." She chuckled. "Maybe I should be happy that he's at least in LA this week."

James pulled his truck away from the curb. "Seems like he's in Vegas a lot lately. Funny that he wasn't there when we were. I don't know if he's experienced Jessie Rae's yet."

"Both he and Kathy are hard at work getting the White Sun ready to open. Tyler likes a good deal, but the building they bought was cheap for a good reason. It needs a lot of work, even before considering all the basic redecorating and remodeling. Both of them are micromanagers, so the work's taking longer than it should." Maria chuckled. "Despite how much he bitches, though, it seems like he's having a good time. I'll admit a lot of that is just about him thinking he's proving some grand point to you."

"Me?" James grunted. "What the fuck do *I* have to do with the White Sun? I know Kathy mentioned something about giving discounts to my guys, but I haven't even driven by the building, and I haven't said shit to Tyler about it."

"The thing is, I think Tyler still can't decide whether he

hates your ass or is grateful to you." Maria shrugged. "He loves competing with you, though. He likes it far more than is healthy. You're a worthy adversary who isn't likely to slit this throat in his sleep. That kind of thing."

James turned at an intersection and frowned. "I'm a bounty hunter. He's an information broker. How are we even in competition? I've done some shit with him, but it was still me doing bounty hunting, and him doing his thing."

"No, you're not getting it," Maria replied. "You don't understand how Tyler views himself."

"How is that?"

She shrugged. "Not as a bartender or an information broker, but as a businessman. You used to be nothing but a bounty hunter who worked alone, and now you have an agency, employees, and influence in two cities and even with the federal government. How many people have a senator who'll answer their calls? You've even got a witch on the payroll, and a hot ex-cop." She grinned. "You're a genuinely successful rich businessman, even if you don't think of yourself that way, and you live in a modest two-story house in a working-class neighborhood."

James grunted.

Maria held up a hand. "Yes, I know you had tons of money from your bounty hunting, but just your last name is scaring most people now, even if Calabrese's guys were dumbasses. No gangs dare to mess with your neighborhood, even though Trey's whole gang spends more time in other parts of LA and Vegas than patrolling their turf. People are more afraid of them as bounty hunters than they ever were as gangbangers. All that influence can and has made a certain man jealous."

"Huh. Never really thought about it that way. Kind of fell into the agency because I couldn't be everywhere at once." James furrowed his brow. "Not trying to be a businessman or piss Tyler off." He chuckled. "Not trying to piss him off with the agency, anyway. Plenty of other times, I *was* trying."

Maria turned to smile out the window. "Sure. I'm not saying it's a bad thing. I think it's funny half the time, and the other half, I like that you've lit a fire under his ass. Plus, the more he expands his business interests, the faster he's going to end up going legit, even if it's by accident. He's not nearly as much of a scumbag as he used to be, if only because the bar's neutrality means cops are always around and he's got to cater to them as well." She laughed. "A little clean ambition is attractive. Don't know if I would have started dating him if he had the same old dingy Black Sun. What can I say?"

James nodded, his hands tightening on the wheel. "Didn't realize all that shit was going on."

"You have to understand the kind of influence you're having on the people around you, Brownstone. Not just Trey or Shay, but the rest of the people you deal with."

"Sure," James rumbled, his thoughts drifting in another direction entirely due to Maria's word choice.

Attraction, huh? Maria's a badass woman and Shay's friend. She might have some good ideas about what would be fucking epic enough for a proposal to Shay. How to ask, though? Shay might know it's coming, but she still wants to be surprised. Got to play this one close to the chest.

James sniffed and rubbed his nose. "So, I was listening to a podcast the other day. It was interesting."

Maria glanced his way. "Let me guess. It was about barbeque."

He shook his head. "It was a relationship one. It's one of the things I do to help me understand Shay better. You women are too complicated." He shrugged. "I wouldn't have to listen to podcasts if you'd just say what you mean."

"Maybe men are too simple, but I see your point." Maria nodded and rested her cheek on her hand. "Shay has mentioned the podcast to me. You're a good guy and a badass, Brownstone, but you're clueless in a lot of ways, so it's probably a good thing you're using any tool you can find to help your relationship. It's one area of life where you can't succeed by applying more force."

"Sure. Yeah. That's the point." James cleared his throat. "So you ever think about your future with Tyler?"

She frowned and sat up straight, looking his way. "What about my future with Tyler?"

"Just, shit, it's a lot to think about." James shrugged. "You were a cop who started dating a crook. You stay at his place a lot, so, you know, gonna move in together sometime, then next thing you know, he's going to take the next step."

Maria blinked several times. "Next step? As in, what, proposing to me?"

"Yeah, yeah. That kind of shit." James nodded. "Ever thought about that?"

This was going well. He could get the information he needed without anything getting back to Shay if he continued with his stealthy interrogation. He almost grinned. He could be subtle when he needed to.

Maria shook her head. "Thought about what? Marriage?"

"Sure, well, no," James replied. "The proposal itself."

She frowned. "The proposal itself?"

He nodded. "Yeah. Like what you want from it, how it's supposed to go down, where. That kind of shit."

Maria's eyes widened. A huge grin spread on her face. "Oh. I see."

James glanced her way.

Why the fuck does she look so excited?

Maria cleared her throat. "You know, I actually haven't thought a lot about it. I've always been so focused on my career that I kind of figured I'd end up with a cop, and it'd be some sort of proposal in the station." She shrugged. "Dated cops, but we just didn't come together. Now, though, I don't know."

"No idea at all? Maybe something fucking epic?"

Maria laughed. "Fucking epic?"

James brought the truck to a stop at a light. "Yeah. Fucking epic. The podcast I listen to has some episodes on proposals, and women are complicated; seems like they want different shit. Some women care more about the ring, others more about the proposal, and others don't care unless it's about the ceremony."

Maria didn't respond for a long moment. The light changed and James accelerated, casting a few quick glances her way.

"Maria?" he asked.

She let out a long, pained sigh. "This isn't about Tyler, is it?"

"Tyler? No? Why the fuck would it be about... Oh shit." James groaned and scrubbed a hand over his face. "You thought I was asking for Tyler?"

Maria crossed her arms and rolled her eyes. "We haven't even moved in together, so taking the next step does seem kind of dumb, now that I think about it."

"Marriage isn't dumb," James rumbled.

She side-eyed him, a grin eating her frown. "Oh, I see. That's what you get for trying to be subtle, Brownstone. You could have just asked my advice and asked me not to tell Shay rather than doing this embarrassing dance."

He rolled his shoulders to loosen them. "It's not like it's really secret or whatever. I kind of tried already, but she cut me off before I could and told me it needed to be fucking epic."

Maria barked a laugh. "Yeah, that sounds like her. If it's not a secret, why didn't you just ask me?"

"I still want the actual proposal to be a surprise, or it'll be fucking weak."

She nodded. "Okay, fair enough. Has she seen the ring yet?"

"What ring?" James furrowed his brow.

"Oh, for fuck's sake. You tried to propose to her, and you don't even have a ring yet?" Maria rolled her eyes. "I get that Shay's non-traditional, but she's still a woman."

"I don't get it," James replied. "So you're saying this is about the ring?"

Maria tapped her forehead. "It's about proving you understand her. Shay's got tons of money. It's not like she needs you to buy her a fancy ring, but you choosing the right ring will help demonstrate that this isn't just James Brownstone bumbling around because of a relationship podcast, but James Brownstone knowing exactly how the woman he wants to spend the rest of his life with thinks."

Shit. Alison didn't mention anything about a ring, but fuck, I shouldn't depend on a teenager to tell me how to do this.

James sighed. "Before it was kind of spur of the moment. I didn't even think about a ring, but you're right —I need something." He shook his head. "Why can't women be more like men?"

Maria smirked. "If women were more like men, I don't think you would be as interested in marrying one, Brownstone." She leaned back in her seat, a relaxed look on her face. "You're making this too hard, anyway. There's no formula here. No recipe. It's not like making barbeque sauce, and no, it's not simple. Women are complicated, so this will be complicated. You'll need to think long and hard about what Shay likes and how to best express your feelings to her while taking that into account."

He nodded slowly, thoughts and possibilities swirling in his head. "Okay, I'll try and do that, but please do me a favor and don't tell Shay I was asking about this shit."

"Sure thing." Maria chuckled. "If anything, I can't wait to see what you come up with and if it surprises her. If there's one thing you do well, Brownstone, it's being fucking epic."

After dropping Maria off, James started the next episode of *The Dude's Guide to Marriage as Explained by a Chick*. It took him a few minutes to figure out how to get a podcast through the console of the truck, though, and then a few more to scroll through the episode list until he found the episode he'd left off on.

Damn it. Really need that new phone.

The last few episodes hadn't been all that helpful since he didn't care about the logistics of wedding planning. He figured Shay could handle that, or they could hire someone. For all he knew, one of the guys in the agency had a hidden talent.

James chuckled at the idea of Lachlan and Manuel planning a wedding. At least it'd be interesting.

"Today's episode focuses on the most dreaded aspect of a wedding," came the soft voice of the woman hosting the podcast. "Something that every man fears and which can lead to massive tension and suffering before the special day happens."

James nodded to himself. This was perfect. Anything they could offer about proposals would help.

"The in-laws and relatives," the woman intoned. "Unless you're very, very lucky, at least one person on her side of the family is going to drive you up the wall. Don't believe what you've seen in romcoms: a lot of them won't come around to your plucky charm and boyish good looks. For the next few episodes, we're going to discuss the different types of difficult family relationships and the best way to navigate this minefield, including key tricks about how to seat people at the wedding to defuse trouble."

James grunted. He was an orphan, and Shay left her

original family behind when she was still a teen. They didn't have to worry about that kind of shit. The family and friends they'd carved out for themselves weren't a bunch of assholes who'd fuck with his wedding, and even if they wanted to, who would screw with James Brownstone on his wedding day?

Yeah, just need to figure out how to propose, and all this shit will fall into place.

He furrowed his brow. Maria had been right, though. He didn't even have a ring. An epic proposal would require an epic ring.

If I were Shay, what kind of ring would I want?

James groaned. If asking around wouldn't work, maybe it was time for a James Brownstone-style approach.

CHAPTER FOUR

Shay glared at her phone, the forum message on her screen producing concentrated irritation in her mind.

Sorry. Don't have anything available like that at this time. You might want to ask around a few tomb raiding forums. Maybe someone could grab that kind of artifact for you. I hear Aletheia's pretty good, if choosy with her clients.

She groaned. Just what she needed: people recommending she hire herself to get the artifacts she needed.

"How can it have been decades since magic returned fully to the world, but I have to jump through hoops to get shit that is probably growing on trees in Oriceran? Why hasn't some damned gnome set up an American Magic Wholesaler's Club or something already?"

The scum swimming around the dark web liked to brag about how they could get anyone anything for the right price, but her attempts to find half-way decent defensive artifacts were slamming into wall after wall.

Shay sighed and laid her head on the back of James'

couch. Her defensive artifacts had been dying out too quickly. Admittedly, she'd put them through their paces by engaging stronger foes more directly than in the past, but what good was a shield ring or a gauntlet that toughened skin if she couldn't use it to take down some magical asshole much stronger than her?

Upping her game as a tomb raider and having James' back meant she needed something powerful and reliable, so she didn't end up getting melted the next time some weird magical being like He Who Hunts showed up and decided to go after her man. She needed a permanent solution, something that would allow her to take punishment closer to what James could handle.

"They're right," Shay muttered. "I'm just gonna have to find some kick-ass armor artifact on a raid. Maybe some less hateful version of Whispy." She chuckled at the thought. Did enhancement symbionts have sisters?

The door clicked and swung open, and James entered with a pensive look on his face.

Shay lowered her phone and raised a brow. "Eating all that meat leave you constipated? Told ya you need more salad."

James grunted and shook his head. He held up a new phone. "Just getting this set up."

"Oh, yeah. Sorry your old phone got blown up."

"Shit happens." James headed to his chair. Thomas was curled up beside it. The bounty hunter looked at her, a knowing glint in his eye. "Something wrong? You looked pissed off when I came in." He shrugged. "More pissed off than usual."

Shay shook her head. "No, just trying to find some

worthwhile defensive artifacts that'll last more than a few fights. I thought the last few rings and that gauntlet I got my hands on would last, but once they actually had to take some damage, they stopped working." She shrugged. "It's starting to annoy me."

"Huh. I'm sure you'll get something figured out." James dropped into the chair. "That sucks. By the way, what do you consider fucking epic?"

Shay smirked.

Not so smooth, and no, you're not getting off that easily, James.

"Lots of things." She shrugged.

"Like what?"

Shay set her phone to the side and folded her hands in front of her. "The collapse of a civilization is fucking epic. Small, big, whatever. Not something you can watch up close and personal, but still epic."

James grunted. "Yeah, sure, I guess. What else?"

"Hmm." She leaned forward. "Dragons."

He frowned. "Dragons?"

Shay nodded. "You have to agree they're pretty fucking epic. At least the grown ones."

James scrubbed a hand over his face. "What about epic Earth shit? Not like we have a lot of dragons around here."

"You didn't say anything about it having to be Earth-based." Shay offered him a mocking grin.

He shrugged. "Now I am. Fucking epic and on Earth."

"Nuclear explosions." Shay nodded and tapped her chin. "Don't want to see one, but everyone has to admit they are pretty fucking epic. A stampede on the Serengeti. A rocket launch, I suppose." She chuckled. "Did you hear they're talking seriously about doing a moon base? A consortium-of-nations thing. It's kind of funny when you think about it. Magic came back, and it's like we forgot about all the epic achievements of non-magical humanity, but now we're finally starting to remember. Don't know if it's just politicians talking, but it'd be pretty badass and epic to have a moon base."

James stared at her, his face twitching. "Nuclear explosions, dragons, huge animal stampedes, rockets, and moon bases? Those are what you consider fucking epic?"

Shay nodded. "It's a small sample of a much larger list. Why are you asking?"

"You know why," James rumbled. "I'm just trying to make this shit simple. Also, what do you want in a ring?"

Shay shook her head. "Let me stop you right there. Nope."

James blinked. "Nope?"

"Yep. Nope."

James groaned. "I don't understand. What the fuck does that mean?"

Shay grinned. "Nothing worth having comes easy. If I just tell you everything, what's the point? I would have thought you would have accepted by now that some things in life are never going to be simple, no matter how badly you want them to be."

He frowned. "You're saying it's some sort of test?"

"That's one way to look at it."

James grunted. "What's another way?"

"Everything in life is a test." Shay smiled. "Don't worry, James. I'm confident you'll figure this out. Whatever else one can say about you, you're not a man who gives up easily." She picked up her phone. "Just like I shouldn't give up."

"On what?"

She nodded at the phone. "On trying to find a more permanent and useful defensive artifact. Not all of us were given free transforming symbionts, but feel free to ask me any more questions. I think you're getting close to something."

James shook his head. "Unless I can arrange a trip to the moon on a dragon that we fly over the Serengeti while outracing a nuclear explosion, I don't think anything you've said will help me."

Shay laughed. "If you could pull that off, it'd go down in history as the most fucking epic proposal ever." Her phone chimed with a message from Peyton, and she looked down at it.

Need to discuss our very special friend from far away.

She looked back up and winked. "I need to go do some shit at Warehouse Two. Keep trying, James. You'll get there."

Shay was still thinking about the conversation with James when she rolled into Warehouse Two.

Maybe I should have brought James along, but he's got a lot on his mind. I'll brief him later. It's kind of cute to see Mr. Bash-Through-Walls try to figure out something that doesn't involve him just kicking someone's ass.

She stepped out of her Fiat once the loading bay door

had closed and headed toward the office. Quick movement in the corner of her eye led to her gun pointing that way until she realized it wasn't an assassin, but a smug-looking orange tabby.

"Watch it, Osiris," Shay muttered. "It's not a good idea to sneak up on me if you don't want to get shot."

The cat meowed once and wandered off in the opposite direction.

"Fucking cat thinks he owns this place."

Shay continued toward the office. Peyton sat inside, frowning at his computer and mumbling under his breath.

She crossed her arms and leaned against the doorjamb. "What did you want to talk about? Is our alien hacker active again?"

Peyton nodded. "I caught the trail of someone who might have been her poking around some DoD servers but lost it. Maybe it's nothing. After all, she hasn't gone after you or James in a big way in at least a month. Heather and I have gotten stuff hardened now. I think she can get through, but she must realize she can't get through without us knowing." A smug smile settled on his face. "In other words, we've beaten an advanced alien. She's probably whining about 'lowly apes who dare defy me' about now." He snickered. "I wonder if she's crying."

Shay snorted. "There's no way she's just going to give up, not after that speech and not after sending those nanites at James." She frowned. "The way she talked, it was almost like she was on a personal mission of vengeance or something. I spent years as a professional killer, and I know the difference between someone killing someone as a job and someone doing it because it's personal."

Peyton turned his chair to face Shay. "You know, I didn't want to bring it up before, but we've got to consider what we've learned, and not just that there's another alien out there who has a thing for throwing cryptids made of nanites at James."

"What are you talking about?" Shay narrowed her eyes.

He held up a hand. "Look, James came here as a scared little kid, but this woman has traveled who knows how far to take him down because of what he is. Maybe that should concern us. It's got some serious implications."

"Like what?"

"I'm just saying maybe she has a good reason to be pissed." Peyton shrugged. "You just said this was personal for her, so we can't dismiss it as her being a bitch for the sake of being a bitch."

Shay snorted. "Or maybe she's some space racist trying to cull the *wrong* type of alien, from her perspective. Maybe her space-racist dad got booted out of the Fascist Star Empire or whatever because he let a few 'impure' aliens escape. It could be personal in that sort of way."

Peyton looked back and forth as if afraid someone else were listening. "James' amulet doesn't come off as the kind of thing made by a peaceful race. It's powered by hatred and anger. That's kind of messed up when you think about it."

She marched over to the chair and glared down at Peyton. "So the fuck what? Even if his people are the worst sons of bitches ever, he isn't them, so I don't give a shit what this bitch's problem is with his race. He grew up on this planet, and his loyalty is to this planet. He's proven that again and again. He's put his fucking life on the line. He didn't have to fight the Council."

Peyton swallowed and paled. "I'm not saying he isn't loyal to Earth. What I'm getting at is, unless he's the last of his race, how do we know some of his cousins won't show up? What if they're not as nice? Before, the whole idea of there being different aliens on Earth might have just been theoretical even with the information we'd found, but the attack in Canada proves he isn't the only one. There could be hundreds or thousands, for all we know. It's easy to hide as an alien on a planet overrun with weird magic, especially when everyone's still getting used to different races. I've been thinking about that a lot myself lately."

"Shit." Shay took several steps back until she hit the wall. She closed her eyes and took a deep breath. "Okay. Sure. It's not like I haven't thought about that possibility, but what good does it do for us to worry? We can't do anything about it. I'm only gonna worry about problems I can solve through force or otherwise."

They stared at each other in silence. Shay's heart pounded. She wanted to punch Peyton in the face for daring to associate James with something dangerous, but it wasn't like she could deny his logic, or even that similar thoughts had crossed both hers and James' mind more than a few times. Hearing someone else voice them so directly unsettled her, though.

"Think of it this way," Peyton began, his voice quiet. "Maria hated James for a long time, right? From her perspective, he was a dangerous, out-of-control monster, but when she got to know him, she came around. She even works for him now. That proves that his enemies can become his friends."

Shay shook her head. "Maria never tried to kill him. It's not remotely the same damned thing. Maria wanted him to go to jail, and it's not like she didn't have tons of opportunities to shoot him when his back was turned, as opposed to Little Miss Wendigo."

"I'm just saying that even if this alien woman's a ruthless bitch, if we can somehow get more information about her, then maybe we can find out more about where James comes from and also make sure he's the only one like him coming here. After everything you and I have seen about Project Ragnarök and Project Nephilim, we both know that if there's another alien like him around who makes any sort of noise, the government will come for James. We don't know anything about this alien woman other than that she hates James and considers him some sort of monster. We need to know more, or hell, maybe we can even get her to back off if she understands he isn't a threat."

Shay snorted. "What's your great plan, then? We're supposed to wait around until she comes at him again with some ridiculous technology we can barely hope to counter? And we don't even know if it's a female." She shrugged. "The alien might have used a woman's voice to try and manipulate me. You keep assuming everything she said was the truth. Maybe it's the opposite."

Peyton blinked. "The opposite?"

"Yeah. Like I said, maybe she's from some fascist galactic empire or some shit." Shay sneered. "Let's say you're a dangerous alien or the scout for a group of dangerous aliens. You come to Earth and start checking things out. It's not so safe for standard invasion because magic's around, so you take it easy, check things out and try to find individuals who are particularly dangerous. After all, you're an advanced alien with nanites. You can probably hard-counter things like missiles, but maybe magic is rarer and harder to deal with."

Peyton shrugged. "We have no proof of that, but I'll admit it sounds plausible. Where does James come into all of this, then?"

Shay clapped a hand to her chest. "Because of that amulet, that 'enhancement symbiont' as it calls itself, you have at least one being on this planet who can remain unaffected by almost anything. Maybe you and your band of planet-invading assholes have run into his species before and they threw back your invasion, so now you're careful whenever you see one."

Peyton rubbed his chin and nodded. "You're saying he isn't from the bad guy race, but her people are?"

"Exactly. Invading asshole aliens wouldn't send a little kid with that kind of potential away. James had no fucking clue about most of Whispy Doom's abilities until this last year. He barely wanted to use the thing and could have been killed. I don't care how bloodthirsty his amulet is—everything about the way he arrived makes it sound more like he was the one running away, or he was sent away." Shay shook her head. "I think that bitch and her friends are chasing down the only real threats to their plans. I wouldn't be surprised if the reason they haven't invaded in a big way is that they don't know how many like James might be around, but obviously he's enough of a problem that she's shown her hand already. He might be the only thing standing between us and an alien invasion."

Peyton sighed. "That all makes sense, but we don't have proof either way. Although when you describe it that way, a lot of things make more sense. Why would his people send him to this planet by himself? Maybe you're right, and he was a refugee. For all we know, his parents shoved him through a portal or something while their planet was being bombarded."

Shay shrugged. "Maybe, but the point is, I'm not gonna trust a single thing that bitch says, and I'm gonna operate only off the facts in front of me. She definitely wants James dead, which means I want *her* dead." She sighed. "But I don't know how to protect James, because I don't know where this woman is or her true identity. And it's like I said —even setting aside the alien shit, she might not be a woman."

Peyton furrowed his brow and worked his jaw a little in thought. "Maybe you don't need to protect James."

"What?" Shay yelled.

He withered under her glare. "I'm just saying James can protect himself. He beat her nanites already, didn't he? Not just that, the guy took down He Who Hunts, half the hitmen in LA, and monsters out of freaking nightmares. And sure, you helped him, but he took down an entire international criminal gang, and a cartel, too. Even before you helped him with the Harriken, he killed an entire damned building full of them by himself." He shrugged. "Just saying, caring is good and all, but your boyfriend is the very definition of badass. If the alien thought she could win against him, she would have come at him again, which means she already took her best shot and failed."

Shay pursed her lips. "Maybe, but even James can bleed, so I need to watch his back."

Peyton turned his chair back toward his computer. "I shouldn't have brought it up."

"No, it was a good thing." Shay sighed. "James isn't a normal man. I have to keep that in mind because it means he doesn't have normal problems. Well, some normal problems, but a lot of fucking abnormal ones."

Peyton shook his head. "You're getting obsessive, just like him. It's because you've been sitting around too much. You haven't done a raid since early January when you and Lily hit that site in Sri Lanka."

Shay shrugged. "So?"

"It's almost March, Shay." Peyton tapped on his keyboard. "It's getting longer between raids."

"I don't need as much money. I'm richer than most CEOs." Shay grinned.

"You aren't meant to be that relaxed. You aren't wired that way." Peyton continued typing. "And if you don't keep your skills fresh, you'll regret it when the time comes that you need them. I think this would be a good time for you to stop obsessing over the alien and focus on something else for a few days or weeks."

Shay shrugged. "It wouldn't hurt to do a job, but I don't want to waste time fetching some magical Viagra or shit like that. If you want to distract me, then I need a serious job, preferably somewhere I haven't done a job yet."

"Why?"

"Might as well experience something new, and it cuts

down on the chance I'll run into someone or some*thing* I've annoyed before." Shay snorted.

Peyton saluted her. "Don't worry, I'll find you something special. Something that has absolutely nothing to do with aliens and is somewhere new."

CHAPTER FIVE

James pushed into the Leanan Sídhe, looked around, and made his way through the thick crowd of happy patrons chatting and downing their drinks. Their voices formed a pleasant din, relaxing and familiar despite the loudness.

The people looking his way parted for him, smiles on their faces. It'd been a while since someone bothered him about participating in another Bard of Filth competition, but the desire burned in their eyes. He could see it every time he came to the pub.

Don't get your hopes up. That shit is never happening again. I'm just here for a little help on a fucking epic ring.

The Professor sat in the back, an amused look on his face and a mug of beer in hand. Only the faintest red touched his face, suggesting that Father O'Banion hadn't come out to play yet.

The tension fled James' body. He didn't want to discuss proposals and rings with the Professor's other self. Some things weren't a joke.

James closed on the old man's table and sat across from him. "Hey, Professor."

"Good evening, lad." The Professor took a sip. "I didn't realize you were coming tonight. You could have texted me. You're lucky I'm here."

"Lucky? You practically live here." James shrugged. "And I didn't text you for a reason. I was trying to do everything I could not to leave a trail."

"Really, now?" The Professor let out a quiet chuckle. "James Brownstone being all mysterious. I'm intrigued. That is so not like you."

James looked over his shoulder as if he expected Shay to be crouched by the bar watching him with AR goggles or using a microdrone right overhead. "I need help getting an artifact. I need someone who can get their hands on one, but who I can trust to keep their mouth shut. You understand?"

The Professor nodded. "Those are qualities I'd attribute to myself." He leaned back, a faint grin on his face. "Why come to me, lad? Are you worried that if you and the lovely Miz Carson go off on another adventure something unpleasant will happen? Even if it did, I'm sure you could handle it."

"No, it's not like that." James frowned. "I'm looking for a ring for Shay, something fucking epic."

"A ring, hmm? Why a ring?" The Professor scratched his cheek, his grin widening. "Ah, I see, lad. Even though I've mentioned it offhand before, I've often wondered when this day would come. You've changed a lot since you've met her. I can't say it's a surprise."

James nodded. "I want it to be a surprise for her. She

kind of already knows because I kind of already tried to ask, and it…" He grunted.

"Not romantic enough, lad?" The Professor sipped his beer. "I can send you to talk to Anna Forsythe again. She knows a little about romance."

"I don't need that Celtic succubus's help." James grunted. "And it wasn't about romance anyway. It wasn't epic enough, or it wouldn't have been. She stopped me before I could even ask." He nodded. "I get that a ring is the first step, but fuck diamond rings. Fuck *any* fancy ring. Shay needs something useful. She's been looking for shield rings and shit, but the ones she's been using keep crapping out on her. I want to get her some kick-ass armor or a shield ring as an engagement ring, or two as an engagement and wedding ring pair. That would be fucking epic."

The Professor set his mug down and nodded as a serious look ate his grin. "I'm surprised, lad. Truly surprised. And it takes a lot to surprise me."

"What?" James eyed him.

The older man shrugged. "You've put a lot of thought into this. What you just said is a damned good idea, and it shows you understand the woman well. I agree that Miz Carson will appreciate something like that a lot more than simple jewelry, no matter how beautiful." He sat back and frowned. "That said, do you think she has any aesthetic preferences?"

James shrugged. "It shouldn't be ugly, although in general, Shay doesn't like flashy shit except for that damned car of hers."

"I'll take that under advisement, but it's not exactly as if there's a magic ring shop out there I can order from, not even on Oriceran." The Professor lifted his mug. "But I will endeavor to find something not horribly gaudy that is also functional for what you described."

"Thanks. I appreciate it."

After another sip, the Professor stared at James. "I'm acting as if it's not a surprise that you're about to settle down, but if you'd asked me even a year ago if I foresaw such a thing, I would have laughed in your face even if I were stone-cold sober. Now here you are, shopping for a ring like any regular man. A magic ring, yes, but still a ring. You even have a daughter already. You're still the Granite Ghost, but you're turning into a genuine family man. It boggles the mind and challenges my perception of reality." He nodded sagely and took another sip.

James shrugged. "Shit happened, and shit changed."

The Professor burst out laughing. "Spoken like a true romantic."

James chuckled. "Besides, I'm not really settling down, at least not yet. Still have bounties to worry about. Shay might be slowing down on tomb raiding, but it's not like she's planning on quitting anytime soon. So, the way I see it, this isn't settling down, it's just both of us getting permanent kickass reinforcements."

The Professor lifted his mug and drained the last few ounces. He set it down. "May the Brownstone Army grow forever more!"

James was halfway back to his house when his phone rang with a call from Sergeant Mack. He answered it on speak-

erphone. He had to admit his new phone was faster and easier to navigate.

"What's up, Mack?" he answered. "I thought you wanted to push back the next PFW meeting until March while we figured out the ratios on some of those sauces?"

Mack sighed. "Yeah, I wish this were about barbeque, but it's not so easy. This is about police business and a bounty."

James grunted. "That's not a big deal. I was still a bounty hunter last time I checked. What's wrong? You get word of a level five coming in soon? I've been kind of bored. I'd be happy to welcome them to LA."

"Nothing like that." Mack chuckled. "It's a level two, actually."

"A level two?" James checked his mirror and changed lanes. "You should just call the agency and have them handle it. I'm not *that* bored."

"Yeah, I get that this kind of thing isn't worth it for you personally, normally," Mack replied. "But this is a special case, and I want to make sure this particular guy gets brought in, even if it is a little like using a sledgehammer to kill a fly."

The F-350 switched lanes as James guided his truck toward a highway onramp.

"What's so important about some level two?" James rumbled. "Even if he's a mob witness or shit like that, Maria, Trey, and the guys can handle it. I've got other stuff to focus on right now."

Mack let out another sigh. "I'm not disrespecting your people, James. I've seen the kind of bounty hunter Trey's become, but this guy has information law enforcement needs. You see, he's got information, but not on the Mafia or some gang or any normal criminal group. It's far different. He used to work for the Eyes.

James grunted. "Fuck that guy."

"Exactly. LAPD, the FBI, and the PDA all want to nail him, but we haven't been able to get in the neighborhood of a warrant because all possible witnesses keep ending up dead, brain-wiped, or worse."

James grunted. "Worse?"

"Six months ago, the FBI got word that someone who worked for the Eyes wanted to roll on his operation. The FBI and the police show up at this house, and the guy's clawed his own eyes out. He's ranting and raving about all the shadow demons tearing through his body." Mack sucked in a breath. "I wanted to spend the next three days in church after reading that report."

"The Eyes summoned demons?" James frowned.

"No. I don't know if that would have been better or worse. From what I've read, there were no monsters there, James, just some residual magic on his brain. They got rid of the magic, but the damage was done. The guy's now a vegetable in a mental hospital, and the few times he is lucid, he still sees the demons. God save that poor man's soul."

"I haven't dealt with the Eyes myself." James grunted. "Everything I've heard from him has been passed to me indirectly through other informants or information brokers. Sounds like a real piece of shit."

Mack cleared his throat. "That crap I just described, that's when he's trying to hurt people, but even normally he's feeding off their minds or something at that stupid dust den he runs. It makes being a junkie look wholesome in comparison. Whatever the hell he is, he's smart enough to have just enough pull here and there, including corrupt politicians and dirty cops, to keep the full force of the law off him. Can't get a bounty since he hadn't been associated with an indictable crime. Our only chance of taking him down is defectors from his organization, and this level two, Julius Carver, is the first one we've come across who managed to make it out of LA before the Eyes blenderized his brain with magic. Julius was in charge of a lot of the Eyes' dark web presence. He has to have dirt on the asshole."

James frowned. "I don't get it. Why didn't the police just offer to protect him? Are you worried about dirty cops killing him?"

"No, not worried about that. We have good solid cops ready to protect him until he can be transferred to FBI and PDA custody. We tried to reach out to Julius, but he blew us off. He doesn't believe the police can protect him, but if you get involved, it doesn't matter. You bring him in, and we'll make sure the Eyes goes down. You and your agency are doing a lot to clean up this town. This is just an extension of that."

James took a deep breath and slowly let it out. "If it weren't for you asking I'd say no, but okay, fine. I need to have the back of my PFW co-captain. I'll bring Carver in. If he's out of LA, from what you said before, you got any idea where he is now? My people and I can start tracking him down, but we need somewhere to start."

"Last information we got suggests he's in Mexico. The

thing is, if we've heard that, the Eyes might have heard it as well, so you're racing him on this, James."

James snorted. "I'll track him down and help you solve your little Eyes problem."

"Thanks, James," Mack replied, his voice thick with gratitude. "Talk to you soon."

The call ended.

Too bad the Eyes doesn't have a bounty. It might have been fun to see how his rep stacks up against mine.

Shay eyed James from the dining room table. "Mexico?"

James nodded, having finished explaining the situation to her.

"He's just a level two, so it'll be pretty easy." He shrugged. "You can come along if you want. This won't be like Alberta. No snow and shit unless we head into the mountains."

She waved a hand dismissively. "Eh, sounds kind of boring. You don't need me to watch your back on a level two. You go do your favor for Mack. Peyton's looking for a job for me anyway, so I might go and do that while you're hunting this guy down. It sounds like it might be annoying and take you a while.

"Maybe, but Mack needs my help." James shrugged. "Okay." He frowned. "Shit, you're right. I don't even know where he is in Mexico. I better get Heather on finding this guy right away."

CHAPTER SIX

Peyton hummed to himself as he looked through a tomb raider message board for possible clients. His bots were patrolling several other boards and forums, but his current choice, nestled deep in the dark web, presented the best opportunity to find something special for Shay.

It'll be good for all of us to stop thinking about aliens for a few weeks. Heather and I have our general defenses locked down in cyberspace, and if the alien chick is trying to hide her attacks as local monsters, she probably won't come at Brownstone while he's in the middle of a major city that has tons of other powerful bounty hunters, AET, local PDA offices, and that kind of stuff.

As far as Peyton could tell, Team Carson and Brownstone had the upper hand in the situation.

He stopped typing to read a job description.

Seeking experienced tomb raider for Cambodian magical artifact recovery job. Extreme danger. Encounters with local magical creatures assured, but no encounters with intelligent beings likely. This is a time-sensitive job. Please inquire immediately if interested.

Encrypted contact information followed.

Peyton chuckled. The description was more straight-forward than he was used to seeing in the dark web, almost coming off more as a regular job offer versus the cryptic rabbit hole of messages he normally had to follow before getting any sort of concrete details about a job.

Osiris meowed from the back of his desk. He was curled up next to the computer, enjoying the exhaust heat. The cat probably thought it was meant to keep him warm.

"I'm guessing this is someone new at the tomb raider hiring game, Osiris," Peyton explained to his pet. "Or someone who is damned confident."

That was the nice thing about having an animal around. When you talked to yourself, you didn't seem as crazy.

"Some rich dude," Peyton continued and nodded. "He's read about something somewhere and wants it, but is smart enough to know that going after it will get him killed. He's going to throw out money to tomb raiders but doesn't care enough to keep himself as low profile as he should."

He leaned back and smiled. This kind of client smelled of desperation, which meant a bigger payday. Nothing wrong with squeezing a premium out of a wealthy asshole.

Huh. I guess technically I grew up a wealthy asshole.

Peyton sent an encrypted message using the contact information.

"I bet this will turn out to be an easy job and Shay will make tons of money while exploring a country she hasn't done a raid in before." He smiled, already satisfied with his anticipated success.

Peyton brought up the forum again to keep looking for

possibilities. He blinked less than a minute later when a response to his message popped up.

"Huh. Didn't expect them to write back so soon. So, what do we have here?"

Peyton clicked on the message to bring it up. He first took a minute to read through various headers and key information to ensure it was genuine before moving on to the message body. Sucker newbies let themselves get distracted by the text before verifying everything else. He'd learned that lesson the hard way years prior.

Sorry. The job is no longer available. Thank you for your interest.

He burst out laughing. "You snooze, you lose, I guess. Damn. Time to find something else special, then. Damn. I wanted to drain your bank account, random rich guy."

James tugged on the knotted rope as Thomas barked and bit down on the other end. The dog yanked hard against his master's playful grip.

"You want this, boy?" James rumbled. "Gonna have to pull harder than that. Show me you want it."

His phone buzzed in his pocket and he retrieved it, keeping one hand on the rope.

James glanced down at the phone before bringing it to his ear and cradling it with his neck. "What's up, Heather? Any luck?"

"I've been trying to track down your bounty. Been hitting a lot of his financial records and accounts, directly and indirectly." Heather chuckled. "I have to say, the guy's pretty good. Better than I expected. Good for him."

"Meaning what?" James allowed more slack in the rope. Thomas' tail wagged hard and thumped against the floor after he backed up and tightened the rope again.

"Meaning that your guy has set up a very clever trail to convince people that he's in Mexico." Heather blew out a breath. "But he isn't in Mexico, I guarantee you that."

James grunted and lowered the rope, his signal to Thomas the game was over. The dog barked a few times before circling and lying down.

"If he isn't in Mexico, where the fuck is he?" James rumbled. "He's not in fucking Canada, is he?"

The clack of Heather typing came over the line. "I can't be a hundred percent sure, but in my experience, if you're looking for someone who is trying very hard to point you somewhere else, you should look less for evidence and more for a suspicious *lack* of evidence."

"And where is there a suspicious lack of evidence?" James stood. He sensed he'd need to head out soon. He'd worried that this bounty might take weeks, but a couple of days wasn't so bad.

"San Diego," Heather replied, triumph in her voice. She sighed. "But this is where it gets annoying."

"What?" James grunted. "How?"

"Annoying for me, not for you. I was very impressed with the false trail, but he got sloppy at the end. I can tell you the exact hotel he's staying at." Heather sighed. "It's fun to beat losers, but I prefer worthy adversaries."

"Send the address to my phone," James replied. "I'm gonna head out right away. This is a favor to Mack.

Doesn't need to be a worthy adversary for either you or me."

He opened his closet and grabbed a shabby gray coat. He eyed his basement before deciding against it. This was a simple bag-and-tag of a level two. The hard part was finding Julius, and Heather had already done that.

Should have run to Mexico for real, dumbass.

James stepped toward the closet before stopping and turning toward the basement door again. "On second thought, might be helpful to grab a few things. Never know who I might run into."

James stepped out of his truck into the parking lot of the seedy motel. He chuckled at the neon sign informing travelers the building was a nice M T L.

Algae had conquered the pool, making him wonder if some sort of Oriceran fish creature now lived in it.

Could make more sense to stay at a fancy place where they'll be better about your privacy when you're on the run. These fuckers always come to these seedy shitholes, and I always find them.

He frowned and wondered if he should bond his amulet before shaking his head and walking toward Julius Carver's room. It was one thing to use Whispy when he was raiding a house filled with dozens of men, but he didn't need an alien amulet to capture a single level-two bounty.

I have some *pride.*

James stopped in front of the door. The blinds were drawn, but he knocked and waited.

No one answered.

He rolled his eyes.

I hate it when they pretend to not fucking be there. How dumb do they think I am?

"I know you're in there, Carver," James rumbled. "And you might as well come with me, because if *I* can find you, someone else far less nice can find you too. Probably the worst thing I'll do is break some bones, not rip out your soul like the Eyes."

"Oh, shit," came a voice from behind him.

James spun. A skinny, balding middle-aged man in a t-shirt and jeans stood there holding a bucket of ice. He stared at Brownstone.

"Hey, Julius." James snorted. "Huh. Guess you really *weren't* home."

"Shit, shit, shit." Julius dropped his bucket and pointed. "Why the fuck...how the hell?" He ran a hand over his close-cut hair. "You're James Brownstone."

"If you know that, then you know how this is gonna go." James shrugged. "If you're thinking some bullshit about how you're gonna be the one who wins against me, that's gonna end pretty painfully for you. Good news is it's not a dead-or-alive bounty, and I hear the cops want to talk to you, so I can't break your jaw or your hands. Might need those to type." He grinned. "Can break your legs, though."

Julius sprinted off.

James grunted and shook his head. "At least the fucker didn't try to fight."

He set off after the bounty but the man was damned

fast, Julius's fear all but giving him wings. A few feet of distance between the men grew to a few yards.

Shit's always harder when you just can't kill the guy.

James reached into his jacket and pulled out a sonic grenade. After a quick prime, the grenade arced through the air.

Julius turned around and yelled, then leapt to the side as the high-pitched whine of the grenade sounded. The bounty groaned, clutching his ears as he slammed to the ground.

Glad Shay convinced me how useful those fucking things are. Not as fun as beating a fucker down, but great in this kind of situation.

James marched over to the stunned man, shaking his head. "You know, if you would have just kept running, you might have been okay. I'm a bounty hunter, not a fucking baseball player." He handcuffed Julius and patted him on the head. "All scraped up, and I didn't even touch or shoot you. What a fucking dumbass."

A few people lingered in the parking lot, taking pictures of James as he stuffed the handcuffed Julius in the back of his truck and secured his seatbelt.

"That's fucking James Brownstone, man," one long-haired man exclaimed. "In the flesh. Scourge of Harriken."

"Shit," replied the man next to him. He pointed at Julius. "That must have been a serious guy, maybe a wizard with the Council or some shit. Damn, we could have all died if Brownstone hadn't shown up."

James chuckled and turned his key. The truck roared to life.

I don't know how people drive electrics. A truck should rumble when it starts. I wonder how long it will be before they ban my truck?

"You can't do this," Julius whined from the back. "I was fucking clear, Brownstone. I was clear. You're taking me to my fucking execution."

James grunted and backed up, the small crowd in the parking lot still standing around taking pictures. "I already told you, dumbass. If I found you, someone else could find you too. That's why you pretended to be in Mexico, right? To throw off the Eyes? Well, it didn't work. You were waiting to get your brain tossed."

Julius sighed. "What are you planning to do with me?"

The F-350 joined the flow of traffic on the street.

"You're a bounty, asshole, and I'm a bounty hunter. I'm taking you back to LA, where I'm turning your ass in for my reward." James shrugged.

Julius groaned. "Why do you even care, Brownstone? I'm a level two. It's all fucking hacking shit. I'm not worth it to you. I get it if one of your boys came after me, but you personally?"

"Sure, but you're worth it to the police, the FBI, and the PDA." James grunted. "Should have taken their protection offer. It would have saved us both time."

"I'm not testifying against the Eyes." Julius shook his head. "No fucking way. If I keep my nose clean and hide out I don't have to suffer, but if he even thinks I'm going to talk to the police, he'll come for me, and I'll be wishing I was dead by the time he's done with me. You don't understand, Brownstone. He's a monster. Not just some pointy-eared elf with cutesy magic or even fireballs. The things he gets off on..." He shuddered. "Please. I'm begging you, Brownstone. If you have any sort of mercy, you'll let me go before the Eyes comes for me."

James snorted. "If the Eyes is that bad, all the more reason for you to spill your fucking guts to the police so they can take him and all the pieces of shit propping him up down. Fuck, if they had a bounty on him, I'd go have a little chat with him myself. I'm really tired of hearing about this guy."

He chuckled.

Wonder if that's what criminals say about me.

Julius let out a crazed laugh. "You don't get it. You can't win against him. He's beyond you. He's beyond mortals."

"What? A pussy who hides in some dark room so he can play at being the boogieman? Yeah, I've heard about him." James snorted. "Even He Who Hunts, who was a crazy, weird motherfucker from who knows where, fought up close and personal. As far as I've heard, the Eyes has a bunch of guards. If he's such a badass, why does he need guards?"

"He isn't like anyone you've ever fought." Julius shook his head. "I don't think he's totally even here all the time. In our reality, I mean. I think he's like split between the worlds or dimensions or something, and when he touches you, it's cold, like the cold of death." He shuddered. "Maybe he's come back from beyond the grave."

James did a quick mirror check. Nothing unusual. He wasn't worried, but there was always the off chance that hitmen working for the Eyes had been waiting for their opportunity. Julius wouldn't do the police any good dead.

"So now he's Death, huh?" The bounty hunter chuckled. "I've never kicked Death's ass before. That might be fun."

"You're going to die, Brownstone," Julius yelled. "But at least you'll die quickly. Please. Just turn around. Fuck, take me to Mexico. Leave me on the other side of the border, and I'll make my way down to Guatemala."

James glanced over his shoulder. "Why not fly to Europe or somewhere?"

"You want me to get on a plane? He'll knock the plane out of the sky." Julius sighed. "The only reason he hasn't tracked me down already is that I got my hands on a potion that conceals me from magic, but it's not going to last forever. You're leading me to my death, and you won't help the cops." He gasped. "I'll cut you a deal. I can pay you a bunch more money; way more than the bounty."

"I already told you this isn't about the money." James shrugged.

"I can...I can...I know! I can give you information on the Eyes' operation. On a thumb drive or something. You let me go, and I'll give you the information." Julius' breathing picked up. "Then your cop buddies can take him down."

"Please." James shook his head and snorted. "And how will I know it's true? Nah. You need to be somewhere the cops can make you verify the shit you're feeding them. We're heading back to LA. Deal with it, Carver. Put on your big-boy underwear. If the Eyes is such an evil fucking freak, you shouldn't have worked for him to begin with."

"You've killed us both, you dumb bounty hunter meathead." Julius slumped in his seat, then threw his back against the door, trying to pull the door open with his cuffed hands.

James laughed. "Yeah, superhacker can't even beat child-locked doors. No wonder you're afraid of your own shadow. If the Eyes wants a piece of me, he can fucking bring it. I'll introduce him to the Harriken and the Council in Hell."

CHAPTER SEVEN

A helpful sign informed James that his exit off I-5 was coming up in a few miles. Silence had ruled the drive back because he didn't want to listen to podcasts with a prisoner in the back, even one who was handcuffed and all but ready to cry. Julius had given up begging for his release after twenty minutes, instead staring out the window with a forlorn look on his face as if resigned to his fate.

"It was a dumbass plan anyway," James rumbled.

Julius kept looking out the window. "What?"

"Hiding forever. You really thought you could pull that shit off?" James grunted. "You should have just figured out a way to take out the asshole yourself. Trust me, I've taken down enough gangs and assholes like the Eyes. It's always the same. Once the head guy dies, they're too busy killing each other or trying to take over to worry about people like you. You'll never be free until he's dead or locked up in some ultramax."

"I don't know if anyone can even kill him," Julius mumbled. "It's like I said. I think he might be dead already."

James took a moment to move his truck into the farthest right lane. "I've killed dead guys before. Shit, I killed a guy who could body swap, so I killed a guy who'd already been dead a few times." He shrugged. "If something exists it can die—simple as that."

"Maybe *you* could kill him." Julius shook his head. "But I'm not you."

"You'll be in police custody soon. If that fucker kills a cop to get to you, AET will come and so will I. Then I'll prove to you how easily he can die."

James frowned as his gaze snapped up to his rearview mirror and then his side mirror. The same two SUVs had been behind him for about thirty minutes and had followed him into the exit lane. That didn't mean anything in and of itself, but they'd followed his earlier lane changes three times already.

Fuck. I should have known this shit wouldn't be so easy. Stupid bounty. You should have just taken a grenade and thrown it at the Eyes and ended all this bullshit before it even started.

A hard turn off the exit took them past a gas station. James accelerated slightly. Getting in a fight around tanks filled with explosive fuel was a bad idea even by his loose standards of what constituted acceptable collateral damage.

The two SUVs kept on him. They passed a few cars and then one hit the gas hard, zooming past James while the other remained behind him.

He narrowed his eyes. "You should be glad you're wearing your seatbelt."

Julius craned his neck to the side. "What's going on?"

"Trouble," James rumbled.

The bounty groaned. "I knew it. It's the Eyes. Fucking Brownstone. You've killed us both."

James snorted. "A badass who can't be killed has to drive around in an SUV?"

"Fine, it's some of his guys—same difference. We're both going to die."

"So we went from the-Oriceran-who-can't-be-killed to worrying about some fucking enforcers who can?" James shook his head. "You really need to grow a pair, and who the fuck knows? A lot of people don't like me. It might just be random assholes who think they're gonna get lucky."

As if connected by a string, the back SUV zoomed forward, and the front vehicle slammed on its brakes. James grunted, tugged on the wheel, and hit the brakes, his tires screeching. The front of the F-350 clipped the front SUV with the sickening wrench of metal, then shuddered a few times and came to a halt.

"Fuck," James growled and slammed his hand on the wheel. "Stay down if you want to live."

Bullets pierced the back and side windows, spreading spiderwebbed cracks over the safety glass. Julius yelled. One of the tires blew, victim of a bullet.

James threw open his door and dropped out of the truck.

Another bullet ripped through the back of the driver's seat and nicked the wheel. James yanked out his gun and rushed toward the back of the vehicle, taking several shots but keeping his head down.

His heart thundered, and he let out a low growl. They'd

done the unforgivable: the fuckers hadn't just dented his truck, they'd shot it up.

Bonding with Whispy would leave him vulnerable for a few seconds. He couldn't risk it, but he did risk a brief glance around the back of the truck to ID the positions of the closest shooters. Several bullets flew by as he yanked his head back. The enemy continued pelting the truck with bullets.

The bullet storm ended, and James took his chance. He stood up and took four quick shots, introducing .45 bullets to the front passenger and driver of the two vehicles. A couple more men sat in the back of the vehicles.

The louder crack of a rifle sounded. A shot blasted through the back of the truck and grazed James' arm. He hissed as blood soaked his shirt, the wound throbbing with each thump of his heart.

The gunfire stopped. James frowned, taking the opportunity to reload. He only had one more magazine in his coat and a single sonic grenade.

Should I try to bond to Whispy?

A bright flash blinded James, and a roar followed. Only a second passed before a fireball exploded on top of the truck, scorching the metal.

The bounty hunter jumped to the side as another fireball arced over the truck and struck where he'd been crouching. The flames licked his side.

His movement sent him clear of the back of the truck and he let loose, finishing off two of the men in the back of one of the SUVs. One of the men dropped a wand he'd been pointing out the window.

"Fucking asshole," James shouted.

He hit the ground with his wounded shoulder and let out a grunt. The bounty hunter hopped to his feet, the burning rage coursing through him dulling the pain of his burns and wounds. His quick toss sent the sonic grenade toward the other vehicle.

The two killers inside threw open their doors and jumped out with yells.

Thought it was a frag grenade, dumbasses?

One of the men screamed with the whine of the grenade. James put three rounds into him and spun to finish off the second assassin, only to find him standing with a smug, satisfied look on his face, a wand in his hand, and the air shimmering in front of him.

"I've heard stories, Brownstone," the man shouted. "Stories about how people threw fireballs right at you and you didn't even have a burn." He shook his head and scoffed. "But look at you now, bleeding and burned."

"You're the only one left alive from your little group, and soon that won't even be true." James fired at the man and the bullet disappeared in a flash.

The wizard backed up, his hand tight around the wand. "Give me Julius and I go away, Brownstone. You don't want to get in the middle of this. I don't even know why you're involved with some pissant bounty like him. It's not your business."

James fired a few more times, the bullets all disappearing. "I've got my reasons. What, am I supposed to walk away because the Eyes is involved? The more I hear about that guy, the more pissed I get."

"Exactly." The wizard nodded. "The Eyes hasn't fucked

with you. The way I've heard it, he has even helped you. You're a little ungrateful, don't you think?"

James holstered his gun and pulled a knife. "You mean by giving information to Kathy but fucking with her about how she could pass it along while He Who Hunts was planning to slaughter families in an amusement park? Am I supposed to appreciate that?"

"He isn't an enemy you want to make. I'm sure he'll overlook all this." The wizard nodded toward his dead comrades. "He's very into survival of the fittest, and you're a survivor, Brownstone."

James threw the knife at the man's head. Half of the blade vanished, but the rest bounced to the ground, hissing and glowing red.

"You know what I think?" he growled. "I think you fuckers just shot my truck up. It's a classic. Parts are hard to find. You even used a fucking fireball."

The wizard threw up his free hand. "Hey, I don't do that kind of magic, so you can't blame me. I'm just here for Julius. Shit, I don't even need his body. Just drag him out so I can verify he's dead and I'm out of here."

James narrowed his eyes, the roar of his pulse quieting. He stepped toward the man, and the wizard stepped backward.

"No," the bounty hunter rumbled, "this is how this shit's gonna go. You're gonna put that wand down and run the fuck away, or I'm gonna kill you. Then I'm gonna march over to Julius and call the damned police, and they'll come and pick him up."

The wizard laughed, but the fear in his eyes undermined it. "You can't win, Brownstone. You can't even hit me. Don't you get it?"

James grinned. "Then why do you look so fucking afraid, and why do you keep trying to get me to leave?" He spread his arms out. "Shoot me, asshole. You just gave a big speech about me being hurt. Fucking finish me off. Become famous as the man who killed the Granite Ghost."

The criminal's face twitched, and his free hand drifted toward his jacket.

James reached slowly for his gun. "You made the same mistake a lot of fuckers do. You assumed that I was tough but a dumbass."

The wizard shook his head. "No. I'm giving you the chance to walk away."

"No fucking way." James let out a low growl. "You run me off the road, and you shoot my truck up. You were dead from the moment you woke up this morning. You just didn't realize it."

The wizard swallowed.

Wait for it.

The wizard went for his gun. His wand dipped, along with the shimmering mass of air, and James pulled his trigger three times. The wizard's body jerked with each shot before he fell backward, gun and wand falling to the ground.

James marched over to the man. The wizard coughed up blood, blinking up at the bounty hunter with shock on his face.

"I've fought plenty of guys with all sorts of magical defenses." James shook his head. "Guys who were only immune to guns, and guys with all-purpose shields. Your problem was that you let me know it was directional. You didn't take a single shot at me with that shield up, and you couldn't hide your fear. I could smell it."

The wizard coughed up more blood. "What the fuck?" he whispered. "Are you a damned wolf or something?"

"Yeah, I'm 'or something.'" James put three more shots into the wizard's head and holstered his gun. "That's for my fucking truck, asshole."

He shook his head and stomped toward the bullet-riddled vehicle. He threw open the back door to find Julius groaning, blood all over the seat.

"You're not dying after all that."

James pulled a healing potion out and downed the contents before grabbing one for a human. He turned Julius over and poured the potion down his throat. The whiner was still breathing, so the magic should be enough to keep him alive.

The bounty's wounds closed, but his face remained pale. "I got shot. It fucking hurt."

James grunted. "Big fucking deal, so did I. Stop bitching about it." He glared at all the bodies and shook his head. There was no easy potion to pour over his truck.

Julius stared at the dead wizard. "Shit, those guys definitely work for the Eyes."

"Yeah, one of the guys said so." James shrugged.

"Fuck my life."

"They're all dead now, so who gives a fuck?" James whipped out his phone. He thought about calling a Currus, but there was still the risk of another attack, so he dialed Mack instead.

The phone rang three times before the sergeant

answered. "Hey, James, I got your text about finding Carver. You almost back?"

James stared at one of the flattened tires on his truck. "I need you to send someone to pick us up. We got ambushed by a bunch of assholes who worked for the Eyes."

"Damn it." Mack sighed. "You okay? What about Carver?"

"I'm fine, and he's fine. He got hit a few times, but I had a healing potion." James growled. "The fuckers shot up my truck."

A car slowed, and the driver looked their way. After a few seconds, he sped away.

What, never seen a bunch of dead guys before? You live in fucking LA.

"I'm sorry. I know how much you love that truck," Mack replied. "I'll make sure a unit comes and gets you."

"Never mind." James watched the car speed away down the road. "I'm pretty sure a bunch of cops will be showing up very soon."

You shouldn't have gone after me in my truck, Eyes. First things first: I'm gonna get my truck fixed, then I'm gonna drive it to your place and have a one-way discussion with you about respecting classic vehicles.

CHAPTER EIGHT

S hay stepped behind her lectern and nodded toward the massive screen displaying an image of the Great Pyramid of Giza behind her. Students and a few professors packed the lecture hall, most leaning forward with eager interest on their faces.

"In conclusion, I want to thank you for taking time out of your busy schedules to attend this lecture on the use of pyramids for energy collection by the ancient Atlanteans." Shay smiled. "If you leave this hall retaining only a few key concepts, please appreciate the malleability of so-called expert historical truth and how the Atlantean imperial efforts, despite their advanced magical techniques, weren't fundamentally different from imperial efforts in the non-magical ancient world. The weapons changed, but the ideas were the same: influence, power, and control. I'd argue that as magic becomes better integrated into modern Earth and technology advances, the same patterns will repeat themselves. Again, thank you for attending."

Light clapping filled the hall for a half minute before

petering out. The attendees rose and filed out, murmuring among themselves.

Peyton's right. The raids are getting farther apart. My excuse for not teaching a regular class was that I needed to keep my schedule open, even if the dean doesn't know about my day job, but maybe it wouldn't be such a bad thing to settle into something more permanent.

Shay was nodding to herself, considering the possibility, when a pale redhead with a chignon and a suit much too expensive for a college professor made her way from the back row. The woman oozed wealth, from her suit to the diamond earrings and a ruby pendant around her delicate neck. The only odd touch was a simple silver bracelet on her left wrist.

Old family heirloom? Doesn't fit with the rest of your outfit, lady.

Despite her expensive clothing and jewelry, the woman's movement lacked the elegance Shay would have expected from a wealthy socialite. There was a confidence in her stride that looked almost military.

Huh. Maybe she's a vet. Pretty face, and smooth. Can't really tell; she could be anything from her twenties to her forties, depending on the kind of plastic surgery or magic she's been using.

The woman continued toward Shay with a slight smile on her face. "Professor Carson, I'm sorry to bother you, but could I have a minute of your time?"

"What did you need? You don't look like a student." Shay looked her up and down. She couldn't recall ever seeing this woman on campus or around the department.

The woman chuckled and rubbed the silver bracelet. A nervous tic, perhaps.

"No, I haven't been a student for a while. My name is Erin North."

Shay furrowed her brow. "Erin North. I've heard that name before, but I can't remember where. Are you involved in archaeology or revised history?"

Maybe she's a rich woman who doles out grants? I should pay more attention in the departmental meetings.

Erin shook her head. "I wear a lot of hats, you could say, but my primary interest lies in running the Global Empathy Foundation."

Shay arched a brow. "Wait, as in that refugee resettlement charity?"

Erin smiled warmly. "Yes. I take great pride in our work. One would think with the return of magic to Earth that humans would stop finding reasons to kill each other, but as long as wars continue and innocents suffer, it's important for those with resources and power to take care of those who can't take care of themselves."

"You do admirable work, Ms. North."

"Please call me Erin, Professor Carson."

"I don't like unbalanced titles. Just call me Shay. Not to be rude, but what do you need from me exactly? I don't think my expertise in history would be very helpful in your work unless you want the depressing news that I think your charity will need to be around until the sun dies."

A brief flash of something like melancholy played across Erin's face. "I don't need to be an expert in ancient history to know that you're right, but my interest in you isn't about the future. It's the past." She pointed at the screen. "Ancient Atlantis, in particular."

"Okay, you've got my attention." Shay grinned. "I do love talking about the past and how we spent thousands of years getting it wrong."

Erin placed her palms together and smiled. "Excellent. Perhaps we could talk over a late lunch? I wanted to discuss the possibility of hiring you as an advisor for a special project, but I have a bit of a quirk where I can only truly get to know a person when I see them eating."

"Not drunk?"

The other woman shook her head. "Not as such. I'm more than happy to pay for wine if you want."

Shay shook her head. "I don't drink during the day. Like to keep a clear head...just in case."

"In case a student surprises you with a question?" Erin raised an eyebrow.

"Among other things." Shay shrugged. "Let's go grab some lunch."

Things have changed when I have socialites instead of hitmen seeking me out.

During the short limousine ride, Erin didn't talk about the job offer. Instead, she focused on relating the successes and failures of her charity, including highlighting the continuing refugee situation all over Earth. Apparently, one of her chief concerns now was trying to reach out to Oriceran for potential resettlement of Earth refugees.

The idea made a strange kind of sense to Shay.

Oriceran had its problems, but they'd demonstrated a better ability to keep things under control than Earth had for most of the last ten thousand years.

The conversation didn't turn away from the charity and refugees until they were at the restaurant and Shay was halfway through her antipasto.

"What do you think about power and responsibility, Shay?" Erin inquired.

Shay swallowed a bite of artichoke heart and shrugged. "What about them? I believe the only thing that keeps people in power responsible is other people with power checking their power. Everything we've learned about Oriceran history reinforces that, too."

Erin picked up her cup of tea and took a sip. "So there's no hope, then? No way to break the cycle? Even with so many intelligent species?"

"I don't know about that." Shay shrugged. "I'm not all that impressed with the so-called intelligence most species have shown, but I can also say that most civilizations have produced grand things in addition to the horrors and wars. Who knows?"

"It sounds to me like you do have some hope." Erin set her cup down and placed her hands in her lap beneath the table. "Perhaps it's simply a matter of dealing with the most aggressive among us. After all, one can look at recent Earth history. Man invented the nuclear bomb and has managed to not use it again."

Shay laughed. "Only because people are afraid of the other side. I don't know if I'd call mutually assured destruction a great example of the glories of intelligence and empathy."

"Mutually assured destruction?" Erin shrugged. "Why not? It arguably kept Oriceran at peace for millennia. That's what you were saying earlier: the only thing that keeps people in power responsible is other people with power."

This woman may be the rich head of a charity, but I can't tell if she's naïve or even more cynical than me.

Shay opened her mouth to respond but closed it. Something in the back of her mind screamed that something was unnatural and wrong. Her killer instincts and tomb raider experience flowed together to kick her heart rate up.

She had slipped her hand into her purse and rested it on the gun inside when she finally realized what it was: silence.

Diners filled the room, chatting, laughing and eating, but she couldn't hear any of it anymore.

Another CIA agent? If so, why the game? I don't see a cube.

Erin tilted her head, a thin smile on her face. "You seem tense, Shay."

"You obviously want a private conversation," she replied, keeping her hand on the gun. "And you have the means to ensure that even in the middle of a public place, which means you're a lot more than some woman running a charity."

Erin picked up her tea and took another sip. "Wealth brings many possibilities, especially in the current world. Yes, I've taken measures to ensure our privacy because I doubted you would follow me anywhere less public, Aletheia."

Shay narrowed her eyes. She considered pretending

she had no idea what the name meant, but if Erin had the technology or magic to hide their conversation and already knew her tomb raider identity, a simple denial wouldn't work. The woman had prepared for the encounter.

"Okay, let's skip the bullshit then, shall we?" Shay snorted.

Erin chuckled. "Ah, the professor has vanished and the tomb raider has come out?"

"Something like that. I take it you don't want to hire me for a historical consultation on Atlantis?"

Shay eased up on the gun. Whatever Erin had planned probably didn't involve a major battle in public. It'd expose them both for what they were, and the wealthy woman had far more to lose than a woman who was officially dead.

The redhead leaned forward, her smile now more predatory than cheerful. "You've made a name for yourself in the tomb-raiding world rather quickly, if you think about it. You're a natural who has shown up other tomb raiders with years more experience, and I need that talent to help me recover an artifact."

"Why the game?" Shay shrugged. "If you know the name Aletheia, you could have contacted me through the internet."

Erin shook her head. "I think I'm a good judge of people. It's useful when dealing with a large international charity. I wanted to look you in the eye and talk to you to make sure you were appropriate for the job. Your reputation for delivery precedes you, but I had to be comfortable with my choice, given the dangers involved."

"Not saying I'm going to take the job or not, but right

now I don't even know what the damned job is." Shay frowned.

"It actually is Atlantean in nature." Erin shrugged. "An Atlantean artifact hidden in some Khmer ruins in Cambodia. They were only recently discovered by remote imaging in the jungle. It remains unclear if they were hidden using magic, but that's a strong possibility."

"What ruins? I pay a lot of attention to that kind of thing, and I haven't heard anything about that."

Erin laughed and shook her head. "You don't understand, Shay. When I say recently discovered, I don't mean months or weeks. I mean days. Some of my money is funding certain space and magical archaeology efforts, so I had access to this information in a timely manner, along with previous information that indicated that an Atlantean artifact had been hidden in that area in ruins that are dangerous; guarded by some sort of magical beasts that were put in the place to defend them."

Shay stopped talking as the waiter arrived with the main course, pan-fried sea bass. He set the plates down, oblivious to the lack of noise.

"Thank you," the women offered simultaneously.

The waiter smiled and departed.

Shay returned her attention to Erin. "What's the artifact?"

"A crystal lance," Erin explained. "A weapon. It soaks up magical background energy to charge itself. According to my information, it was discharged a few thousand years ago and then became all but dormant, but with the return of full magic to Earth, it's had decades to charge itself to unusual levels of power again."

"Some sort of WMD?" Shay frowned.

The other woman shook her head. "No, not as such. It's more that with increased charge, it gains the ability to pierce greater defenses. My understanding is that it was more a tool of assassination. Even the most powerful magical defense would fail after a few years of charging, and this thing has had thousands of years at low power and now decades at full power. It's effectively an unstoppable weapon, and I worry about it being used to kill a prime minister or president or even an Oriceran leader, regardless of their magic. It might be used as a tool to plunge the worlds into more war in the wrong hands." She frowned. "And the last thing either world needs is more war. More refugees." Her face darkened. "I will do what is necessary to stop that."

Erin leaned back, a distant look in her eyes.

Shay sighed. "You have a lot of money. You could send a whole team into those ruins."

Erin shook her head. "We both know an improperly prepared team will get themselves killed. I've done my research, and your name has come up repeatedly. I need someone who I know won't sell this thing to the highest bidder and also has the skills to get it. Not only that, I need someone who can move before it's too late."

"What's the rush?" Shay shrugged. "I hadn't heard about this site, so I doubt most other tomb raiders have."

"If only that were true." Erin frowned down at her fish, anger in her eyes. "My information suggests the United States government is seeking the lance. They're employing a contractor, a mercenary tomb raider named Francois Durand. He's definitely receiving guidance and payment from the American government, but it's been hard for my people to find out much about him or his goals. Some of the previous artifacts he's gone after don't seem all that powerful, from what we can tell." She looked up. "That lance can't be given to any government. At least with nuclear weapons, other people had nukes. There is no mutually assured destruction in this scenario."

Shay stared at Erin, her heart thumping. Francois Durand. She knew the name well. He wasn't just any contractor. He was specifically helping the anti-alien projects Ragnarök and Nephilim, and for all Shay knew other, similar government efforts as well.

Why would Durand want the lance? Is it alien?

Erin steepled her fingers. "I should explain that this isn't the first time I've taken artifacts out of circulation. I've destroyed what I can and hidden others throughout the world. Something about this one in particular worries me though, maybe just because I can't find anything on this man Durand. It's like he's a—"

"Ghost?" Shay interrupted.

Erin nodded. "Exactly. It annoys and frustrates me, so I'm taking additional precautions."

"I've dealt with Durand before." Shay leaned forward with a grim expression on her face. "He's dangerous. I should let you know that if you get involved in Durand, even indirectly, it might end with your life being threatened."

"I don't care." Erin shrugged. "You haven't read much about me, have you, Shay?"

"Not really. I don't pay attention to charity." Shay shrugged.

"There have been four assassination attempts and a half-dozen kidnapping attempts." Defiance filled Erin's eyes. "But I'm wealthy and influential. I have the means to protect myself. Little girls in war-torn countries being carried to safety by their fathers while horrible marauders destroy their cities and shoot those attempting to flee don't have that kind of wealth and influence. Someday I may fall to an assassin's bullet. So be it. Until then, I will protect those who can't protect themselves." Erin locked eyes with Shay. "There are many wolves in this world, Shay, but most people are sheep. Someone has to be a shepherd."

Shay blinked a few times.

She's a damned fanatic, but is it such a bad thing to be obsessed with helping people? Not the way I would choose to spend my life, but at least I know it'll be easy to sleep after the job.

Erin leaned back and took a deep breath, her face as pale as ever but fire in her eyes. "Forgive my intensity. We all have our place in the grand scheme of things, and I feel strongly about what I do for a living. I've sifted through a number of possible candidates for this task, Shay. You're the only one who has the combination of skills, knowledge, experience, and moral fiber I need."

"Moral fiber?" Shay chuckled. "You don't know me as well as you think."

"All I needed to know is that Aletheia is choosy about her clients. That has to mean something." A pained smile took over Erin's face.

Shay shrugged. "This isn't how I usually do things. I need to check out some information on my end before I agree to anything."

Erin nodded. "I understand that, but this is very time sensitive. My information suggests Durand is on the move."

"Twenty-four hours," Shay replied. "I need that much time."

"Very well then, Shay." Erin smiled and nodded at the fish. "I'll send you additional information after the meal."

CHAPTER NINE

S hay paced back and forth in front of the office in Warehouse Two, her arms crossed. Osiris followed her as if she were the most entertaining cat toy in existence.

"She offered you forty million dollars to recover the lance?" Peyton laughed. "She could send an entire mercenary company into the ruins for that much."

"She just dropped that little bit at the end of the meal." Shay shrugged. "She seems convinced it needs to be a tomb raider, not mercs, if only because she doesn't trust mercs based on a few comments she made. Not sure if it's because she blames them for making civil wars worse or doesn't trust them in general."

Peyton shrugged. "Would you trust someone like Grayson to go into a cave and get a weapon?"

"No, but it was almost like she was desperate."

"She probably was, with Durand on the way," Peyton replied. "She's found out enough to know he's trouble and going after the artifact, and he isn't going to bury the lance in some bog where no one can ever use it."

Shay shook her head. "What about the information she supplied? Are we sure she's Erin North?"

Peyton nodded. "Either that, or she's copying her almost exactly, including her online presence and that kind of thing."

"Maybe the little rich woman is more than she appears. Shit. Everyone is. No reason she should be an exception."

"Sure, but at the minimum, her background seems to match everything we'd expect, other than her approaching you directly." Peyton shrugged. "The thing is, my initial checks back up everything she's told you about herself. She inherited a bunch of money, then made a ton more off investments and convinced several other rich people to give money to her refugee foundation. The main negative things I can find concern her hiring teams to rescue people in violation of the local laws of some of the war-torn nations. The US government fined her for sending merce-naries to defend a refugee caravan about five years back, but it was a slap on the wrist. Best I can tell, it's less that she stopped doing it and more that she got smarter about using shell companies to hide it when she does that sort of thing."

Shay frowned. "That means she is willing to use merce-naries when it suits her purposes then, despite her apparent distrust for them."

"Yes, and you're not the first tomb raider she's hired." Peyton entered a few commands, and a page filled with names and artifacts appeared on his screen.

"Anything happen to those tomb raiders? Mysterious disappearances or deaths after working for her?"

Peyton shook his head. "Just the normal spread you'd expect of tomb raiders. Some of them have died and a few have ended up in jail, but most of them who have worked for her are still on the job."

"Why me, then?"

He tapped the screen. "None of the tomb raiders she's used in the past have anywhere near your rep, and they didn't recover any artifacts of major power or importance." He chuckled. "You should be happy. You've got an elite reputation, so this woman wants you to help her find this lance. There are worse things than some charity-obsessed billionaire thinking you're good at a job."

Shay snorted. "So she's some rich saint? No such thing. I'm not necessarily gonna turn down the job, but I want to know her angle before I risk my life. Especially since Durand's involved and she didn't mention anything to suggest this is about aliens."

Peyton shrugged. "Don't know what to tell you. That said, there's definitely suspicious stuff. A lot of the original records from her early life have been lost, and everything else indicates a normal, boring life, private school, elite college—that kind of thing. The missing records aren't super-weird in and of themselves, but they were different records from different agencies, and if you weren't carefully looking at date stamps and digging into things with our kind of paranoia, you might not even notice." He frowned. "It's the kind of thing you'd do if you were leaving your life behind and starting over. It's hard to cover all your tracks, which both you and I know all about."

"So she isn't a perfect saint. She has a past." Shay looked down at the floor as she paced. "What's she hiding? Maybe she murdered some socialite and took over her identity?"

Peyton nodded. "It could be. You could ask her for a DNA sample, but we both know how easy it is to manipulate results, so not much point. You seem really into this, though. Is this about her surprising you at the restaurant?"

"Partially, yeah. If she had said she was CIA or something, I would have understood, but my instincts tell me there's more to her." Shay stopped pacing and frowned. "She doesn't carry herself like a rich woman. She radiates…" she made a circular gesture, "intensity and confidence. It's like if I had pulled my gun on her, I wouldn't have been surprised if she pulled a gun herself."

"Nothing wrong with a little confidence." Peyton grinned. "I'd be confident if I were a billionaire."

Osiris waited a few seconds before bounding off, bored with stationary Shay.

She shook her head. "No, not like that. There wasn't the same kind of sociopathy there. There's also something familiar about her, but I don't know what. Don't recognize the face or the voice. It's like… I don't know how to explain it." She shrugged. "She isn't hard enough to be more than some rich woman. Damn it." She threw up her hands. "The money would be nice, though. You might be right. It could just be that I'm bugged that this woman figured out I'm Aletheia and I never even had her on my radar before. I don't like being surprised."

"If it makes any difference, I don't think she's a secret witch or anything." Peyton rubbed his chin. "My working theory is that she's the daughter of a former crime lord or something like that. She grows up in wealth, not appreciating that Daddy's making his money from arms sales and trafficking. One day she realizes what's going on and loses it. She's the daughter of a monster, so maybe she kills Dad or just waits until someone else does. Takes his money. Starts over. Pledges to make up for the evil she grew up around, feeling guilty the entire time because she lived in luxury off all that dirty money."

Shay laughed. "You should write novels with that imagination. Do you have any proof to back that elaborate theory?"

"Actually, I do." Peyton grinned.

Shay arched a brow. "Seriously?"

"Yeah. Around the time Erin inherited all her money, Gordon Anderson, a major European arms dealer, disappeared. He was from Scotland, but he was living in Malta at the time."

"Anderson?" Shay frowned.

Peyton held up a hand. "Absolutely no relationship to Alison's biological father. Just a coincidence. It's not a rare name."

Shay snorted. "This many coincidences make my eyes twitch."

"You should have a doctor look at that. Anyway, this guy, Anderson—he was a billionaire from arms sales, both magical and conventional. The asshole never met a dictator or a rebel army he didn't want to sell all sorts of nasty weapons to. I even saw a couple of articles that suggested his disappearance and likely death may have saved millions of lives because it disrupted the supply chain for multiple factions involved in several brutal civil wars. More than a few spy agencies tried to assassinate the guy."

"And they never found the guy? Even a piece?"

Peyton shook his head. "Nope. He disappeared. Erin came into her money not long after that. I haven't proven it came from that because it'd take me more than a few hours to hit some billionaire's ten-year-old records to see if she hid where her money came from."

Shay shrugged. "I don't know. She sounds American, not Scottish. Being a redhead doesn't make her Scottish, and if the CIA, GRU, or MSS wanted to take him down, maybe they did. It's not like they'd go on the internet and crow about his assassination, especially if it took place in a different country."

"I know," Peyton replied. "I'm just saying some of the evidence fits my theory, and it'd explain why she's so laser-focused on helping refugees. She's consumed by guilt."

"So we might be dealing with a self-righteous avenger who wants to spend the rest of her life making up for her father's mistakes?" Shay started pacing again. "If she has any true inkling of my past, she might want to take me out when this is all over."

Peyton frowned. "Why? You've turned over a new leaf. If she's gotten into your background at all, she has to understand that."

Shay laughed and stopped walking. "I think I've killed more people as a tomb raider than I did as a professional killer."

Peyton snort-laughed. "Sure, but you don't go out of your way to do it now. If the woman is who I think, I doubt she'd come to you if she thought you weren't alike in some way." His smile drifted away. "The coincidence about the disappearing Cambodian job is too much, though. That had to have been her. I don't understand why she pulled the job."

"I've thought about that too." Shay shrugged.

"Maybe after doing additional background research, she decided you were the only possible choice and gambled on you accepting." Peyton scratched his chin. "I didn't mention Aletheia during my initial contact, so it's not like she just assumed you'd take the job."

Shay chuckled and shook her head. "It's almost like when I first started double- and triple-checking clients and trying to make sure I wasn't going to get ambushed. I used to think every waiter in a restaurant might be a hitman, but now I'm giving public lectures and telling people other than James about my real background. When did I stop being paranoid? I forgot how exhausting it is."

"Enjoying life isn't such a bad thing." Peyton turned in his chair and typed a few commands. "Speaking of old times, it's been a long time since you've had people other than the Professor approach you directly. I'm half-intrigued and half-insulted that she could find your true identity without me becoming aware of it, so don't get me wrong—I'm a little annoyed by this situation too."

Shay furrowed her brow. "Setting her past aside, were you able to verify anything else about the job? This might be pointless if there are no ruins for me to raid."

Peyton nodded. "There's definitely a newly uncovered site in Cambodia and some recent buzz on the dark web about people planning expeditions to check it out, most of it from the last twenty-four hours. A lot of people aren't convinced that the withdrawn job offer means anything. I have found a few references to the crystal lance and it being Atlantean in origin, but the best I could do on short notice was find evidence that it was in North Africa a couple thousand years ago. Nothing to connect it to Cambodia."

"And Durand? Any sign of him?"

Peyton sighed. "If he's involved, he's keeping a clean trail, but that's not new." He rolled his eyes. "But it's not like he's hacking us, so he isn't better than me."

Shay smirked. "I care less about your one-sided big-dick contest with him and more about any information on strange symbols that might be Atlantean or Oriceran in conjunction with the lance. I've yet to run into that guy when aliens weren't involved."

"Nope. Everything suggests it's an Atlantean artifact from way back. There's even supposed to be ancient Atlantean writing on it."

Shay scoffed. "And we've found evidence of possible non-Oriceran aliens from hundreds of millions of years back."

Peyton shrugged. "Sure, but I'm just telling you, there's no evidence that this artifact is that kind of alien. It's Oriceran and was brought over when the portals were previously open, best I can tell on short notice."

Shay sighed. "I'd dive into this shit at Warehouse Four, but we don't have a lot of time. But if you're right, why the hell is Durand interested?" She shook her head. "There has to be an alien connection—something we're just not seeing yet. It wouldn't be obvious from a surface check."

"Maybe, or maybe Durand is just doing a side job. Or

for all we know, there might be an alien artifact in the ruins besides the lance." Peyton nodded at his computer screen. "Erin's job offer might just be a rare case of you getting a little bonus. You can embarrass Durand, make a shitload of money, and get a dangerous artifact away from an asshole you don't like anyway."

"I suppose," Shay replied. "But I'm still concerned that she knew to approach me and that I was Aletheia. That means I'm not keeping as low a profile as I should."

"She's a billionaire," Peyton replied. "She has resources that even a lot of government agencies can't easily access. Does it bother me that she took us by surprise? Sure. But she also didn't paradrop in a bunch of mercenaries to kill us or knock on the warehouse door, so we're still decently hidden." He sighed. "I wonder if it's that important for you to keep such a low profile anymore. Same thing I've been thinking now that my family situation's been taken care of. If I keep edging out of the shadows, in a few years, I might even be a real boy again."

Shay frowned. "Yeah, but you only had one asshole after you, and we've taken care of him. I've got a lot of assholes after me. I can't afford to edge too far out of the shadows."

"Yeah, you can. You don't have a lot of assholes after you at all." Peyton brought up a new article. Erin smiled back from the screen, a beautiful emerald green gown highlighting her pretty face.

The headline read, ERIN NORTH PLEDGES NEW RESOURCES TO MICRONESIAN RESETTLEMENT EFFORTS.

Shay stepped into the office. "Yes, I do. I'm the one getting shot at all the fucking time. It's not something I forget the minute I return to LA. What the fuck are you talking about when you say I don't have people after me?"

"You need to sit down and think about it." Peyton shook his head. He didn't respond for a moment as he scanned the article. "The cartel that wanted you dead is gone. Kaput. History. I get that they weren't the only reason you faked your death, but they were one of the main reasons."

"They weren't the only ones who wanted to put a few bullets in me."

"Who? Snegurka is gone, and if she were going to magically pop back up seeking vengeance, you or Lily would have run into her by now." Peyton shrugged. "The Hollingsworth guys don't hold those kinds of grudges. Sure, you've pissed off a few people here and there, but the nastiest people who actually might have a shot at actually taking you out are all dead. Not only that, your boyfriend is one of the single most badass men in the world, so even if they *can* track you down, that's got to play into their calculations."

Shay frowned. "I don't know if it's as tidy as all that."

Peyton spun his chair to face her and shrugged. "There's nothing inherent in being a tomb raider that requires you to hide your identity 24/7." He shook his finger at her. "You did that because of your past as a killer and the holdovers, and you can still keep that past buried, even if you live a little more openly."

"Sure, but I'm also not exactly obeying the law when I go into some archaeology site and take an object without all the proper permits, even with some of the expanded international magical salvage laws. Do you think the Cambodian government would be very happy to know that I might fly in and take an ancient artifact without even checking in with them?"

Peyton sighed. "I guess that's true, but my point stands. You don't have to worry about Aletheia as some impenetrable secret identity. I think plausible deniability is enough."

"When you're regularly hitting the field more, we'll talk about whether I should worry about people coming after me. If anything, I need to maintain at least a fig leaf of anonymity if I want to do more at the college." She shrugged. "Especially if I want to move beyond guest lectures into something more permanent."

"*That's* what bothering you?" Peyton chuckled. "Your path to tenure?"

Shay smirked. "A dean can be scarier than the head of a cartel."

CHAPTER TEN

What a fucking annoying day, James thought.

A cop waved from the front of the cruiser as he pulled out of James' driveway. Julius had been delivered successfully to the police and the F-350 had been towed to the body shop for repairs, but that left him without a vehicle and an upcoming explanation to deliver to Shay.

He clenched his fists and took a deep breath. From the mechanic's initial checks, most of the damage to his truck was cosmetic, albeit extensive. The engine had miraculously escaped damage, but the transmission needed a little work.

Fucking Eyes. This shit isn't over yet. I'm gonna wait until my truck is fixed, then I'm gonna drive it over to your place, kick in your door, and drag your invisible ass outside before I beat you down. If you have a car or a truck or magic carpet or whatever, I'm gonna blow that shit up, too.

James stomped toward his porch and let out an annoyed grunt as his phone rang. He yanked it out, expecting it to be from the body shop, but it was the Professor.

"Hey," James answered, trying to suppress some of the anger in his voice.

"About the matter we discussed the other day, lad," the Professor began. "I found something that I think would be perfect. An older ring and pendant combination that provide powerful shielding from most forms of magical and regular attacks. Stylish without being gaudy. A nice combination indeed, which is fortunate because so many wizards back in the day had awful taste."

"Finally, some fucking good news."

The Professor laughed. "Bad day?"

"More annoying than anything. Some fuckers did something they shouldn't have."

"Are they still around?"

"No." James grunted. "But their boss still is, and I'm gonna need to handle that situation soon." He turned toward the street with a frown, watching a few cars drive by. "Before we go forward, I want to discuss payment. I'm not doing another Bard of Filth competition, so don't ask. That shit was once in a lifetime, and I was lucky nobody recorded me."

"I'd argue it was more fear than luck, lad, but I see your point."

"So no Bard of Filth?" James rumbled.

The Professor chuckled. "Oh, no, of course not. If anything, I want to wait a long time before I again witness James Brownstone doing such a thing. I'm sure I can get you to agree again at some point." His gulp of beer was audible. "The rareness of the event makes it that much more valuable."

"Meaning what? You plan to advertise it better next time or some shit?"

"Not at all," the Professor replied, deep amusement infusing every word. "The Leanan Sídhe has regulars, a family of sorts. There's no reason to encourage outsiders to come. The atmosphere there is perfectly balanced as it is. They should be rewarded, not anyone else."

James thought that over. It didn't sound like the Professor was planning on fucking with him after all.

"Then we understand each other," he replied. "I'll owe you a favor if you want. Got a more open schedule these days because of the agency."

"A banked favor isn't necessary in this case, lad," the Professor replied. "I want to take your services up front, but it'll be simple and convenient for you. I know how much you prefer things that way."

James snorted. "Yeah, what I prefer and what the world gives are two different things. How simple can it be?"

"Quite. I'm going to have your items delivered via courier. Do you remember Miss Endo?"

"I never forget anyone," James replied. "And she was kind of flashy, so she stands out even more. Am I gonna have to use some fucked-up passphrase?"

The Professor snickered. "Yes. That's the way Miss Endo works."

"Whatever." James frowned. "So do I have to drive to Seattle?"

"No, no. Despite the business we did there before, she

doesn't live there. She'll be bringing your items all the way to LA, along with a few other things for me, and that's where I need your help. I won't bore you with the details, but there's a decent possibility that there will be trouble during delivery. While Miss Endo is resourceful, she's a courier, not a class-six bounty hunter, and some bad men will likely attempt to waylay her and take the items she has to deliver to me."

A good old-fashioned beat down—James could get behind that as a payment easily.

"So go pick up my stuff and kick the ass of anyone who shows up looking for trouble?" James asked.

The Professor chuckled. "Aye, lad. Like I said, simple and convenient. Oh, the only other thing is that this isn't going to happen in the next day or two. I'm presuming, given that you were still looking for a ring, that a proposal wasn't imminent."

James grunted. "Not a problem. Yeah, still working the actual proposal idea, and until I have it down, I don't need the ring. This won't work with just violin shit in some Italian restaurant."

"Truly a romantic. You could teach the poets a thing or two."

"Don't really give a shit if it's romantic as long it makes Shay happy," James replied.

"Then there actually is some hope for you." The Professor sucked in a breath. "But, excellent. I can't tell you how much confidence you agreeing to pick up all the artifacts fills me with. I'm sure Miz Carson will enjoy the ring and pendant, and your help is much appreciated." The Professor paused for a long moment, likely drinking more beer. "And this has saved me the trouble of having to ask for your help. I'll let you go for now, James. I'll talk to you when I have a firmer timetable."

"Yeah. Fine by me."

The Professor hung up, and James stared at his phone.

Shit. Once I have that ring, the pressure is on.

"Understanding and empathy are the keys to a relationship," the podcast hostess explained. "They are the foundation of everything. Even if all other aspects of a relationship, whether intellectual, social or sexual, are being fulfilled, a lack of mutual understanding and empathy will lead to a strained relationship at risk of collapse at the first significant test."

Significant tests? We've had all sorts of tests. Shay doesn't even care that I'm not human. Am I overthinking this proposal shit?

James leaned back in his recliner, his eyes half-closed as he listened.

No, she's the one who told me she needed it to be fucking epic.

"And that same idea extends to relationship milestones such as marriage, children, and buying a home. Listen to what your partner says, but also anticipate their needs. If they've gone to the trouble of clearly articulating their needs, don't dismiss them even if they seem unreasonable to you at first, since you may be failing to use your understanding and empathy to see things from their perspective. What appears difficult might become practical and lead to a great bonding opportunity if you simply approach the request from a different angle. Worry less about the direct request; instead, try to determine the mindset that led to the request and tailor your response to that."

So you're telling me it only needs to be epic and not fucking epic?

James grunted. He could work with that. With the Professor having a line on a practical but useful ring, he was off to a good start, especially given what Shay had been saying about her artifact needs.

He looked up as the door swung open. Shay stepped inside, frowning.

Damn. Not a good time to ask her about epic shit again. Wonder if something annoying happened at her lecture? Should I offer to go threaten the bastard? Not like I would actually have to beat anyone down.

Shay slammed the door behind her and walked over to the couch. "I've got a job prospect to tell you about. Highest pay I've ever been offered, but if I do this job I'm gonna want you to come along, and this definitely won't be a vacation." She shrugged. "Good news, though, I'm pretty sure our main obstacle won't be nanites pretending to be a Wendigo."

Shay finished explaining the job offer and what Peyton had already uncovered.

"Shit." James grunted. "Durand, huh? You should take the job just to finish that asshole off. He's gonna be trouble sooner or later."

"Yeah, I think so, too." Shay shrugged. "There are still a lot of unknowns, which is why I want you to come along.

Erin's too self-righteous, and I'm half-convinced she's throwing me at this because she thinks that at the minimum I'll take out Durand, even if I get taken out as well. Maybe this is just a stall before she can get a bigger team together."

James shrugged. "Maybe, but we know the guy's involved, so he shouldn't be able to get the drop on us."

"We might be able to get some more information on you as well." Shay sighed. "Even if Erin's clueless about aliens, that doesn't mean there aren't alien artifacts there."

James shrugged. "If we find out more about me, fine. If we don't, also fine, but I've got some important shit to take care of first, and that requires a few other things. So can we do this shit in a couple of weeks?"

Shay shook her head. "No, since Durand is sniffing around, we'll need to move on this quickly. If I'm gonna do the job, we should fly out as soon as possible, as in tonight. Peyton can get us tickets while we're on the way to the airport."

James frowned. "You don't understand. That shit with Julius got...complicated, and there's some other stuff I need to handle because of that. It's important."

Shay's brow lifted. "Complicated? How?"

"Some thugs ran my truck off the road and tried to kill Julius." James took a deep breath and looked down. "During the fight, the F-350 got shot up and firebombed. It's pretty fucked up. Not as badly as when my house got blown up, but, it's gonna be out of commission for a few days or maybe a week."

Shay sighed and shook her head. "Some assholes never learn. I'm assuming you killed the guys responsible?"

James nodded. "Yeah, but they were just the errand boys. I need to take down the fucker who sent them after me."

"The Eyes?"

"Exactly." He let out a low growl. "This wasn't personal before. Now it is, and he needs to answer for what he did. People need to understand. It's why no one comes after my fucking house anymore. They saw the kind of shit I did when someone took it out." He frowned. "Slowing down on bounties I'm handling personally means fuckers don't always think before they decide to mess with me."

Shay shook her head. "Some people are just dumbasses, James. Don't overthink it."

"It doesn't matter. They fucked up my truck on his orders, so now I'm gonna fuck him up. Simple as that."

Shay laughed. "Well, from what I've heard, there is a long list of crimes that come before him fucking up your truck, but I get it." She walked over to him to take his hand in hers. "I've totally got your back, and if you want to raid this asshole's place I'll crack out the *tachi* and slice him in half myself, but it's gonna have to wait. I can't risk Durand scoring an artifact ahead of me, let alone an alien artifact, and it's not like I'm so rich that forty million dollars is easy to blow off."

James frowned and crossed his arms. "You told me about going into ruins, but you didn't tell me where. February isn't that much warmer than December in Canada. Is this going to be more snow shit?"

Shay shook her head. "No to Canada. It's in Cambodia. I checked the weather earlier, temperature range the last few days has been between low seventies to high eighties.

If the ruins extend underground, it will probably be in the fifties, depending on how deep they go into the ground. Not bad. Just normal."

"Cambodia?" James grunted. "That's a decent plane ride even on a supersonic."

Listen to what your partner says and anticipate their needs.

He sighed. "Fine, but we're gonna talk to the Eyes the minute we get back. That fucker's gonna get a lesson about respecting classic trucks."

Shay nodded. "Sure, James. If you want, I can use some of the payment to hire a bunch of mercenaries to invade his club." She smirked. "That might be fun, actually."

James shook his head. "I don't need to hire people to do my ass-kicking. Some things require the personal touch." He slammed his fist into his palm.

Shay pulled out her phone. "I'll let Erin know and have Peyton secure the flight. Grab what you want from the basement, then we'll hit Warehouse Three to grab everything else we might need." She winked. "Don't worry about the Eyes for now. Think of it as something to look forward to."

CHAPTER ELEVEN

The Land Rover shook and bounced as they sped through the thick undergrowth. James had slept on the plane, having wonderful dreams of laying waste to the Eyes' club as revenge for his truck. Now, as they barreled toward the Khmer ruins, he found his mind drifting back to proposal possibilities.

Something on a tomb raid. That's all about sharing her interests and shit. Maybe the Professor could help me find something. Would that be romantic? Fuck if I know.

His gaze cut back and forth as the trees zoomed by, the occasional bird taking flight. They sped past several fallen banyan trees, the trunks lining both sides of their path. Leaves and branches were crushed into the ground between them.

"You see what I see?" James rumbled. "It's gotten more obvious the last few miles."

Shay frowned and nodded. "Someone's been this way already, and recently."

Despite it being early in the morning, the thick canopy

overhead blocked most of the sunlight struggling to make it through the thick clouds covering the sky. It left a stark contrast between dark shadows at the base of many of the trees and the lighter bands between, like an extended twilight.

"Better stop for a second and bond Whispy," Shay suggested.

"I'm fine," James replied.

Shay snorted. "Don't think I didn't notice the blood on your clothes the other day when you came home." She pulled a ring out of her pocket. "Only got two of these left, but that should be enough for this raid—assuming we don't run into something ridiculous."

She slipped her ring on and muttered an incantation under her breath. A golden aura bathed her body, highlighting her face and eyes. The tactical vest and AR goggles atop her head might have undermined some men's vision of what perfect beauty was, but James liked the idea of his personal and gorgeous Angel of Death sitting right next to him.

James eased off the gas and let the Land Rover slow to a stop. He took a deep breath and reached under his shirt to pull the spacer off his amulet. The tendrils shot through him, not even bringing a grunt despite the burning sensation of something digging through his chest.

Initiation, Whispy sent.

James finally grunted. Whispy had his uses, but now the bounty hunter would need to keep his thoughts disciplined. Having someone else in his head was annoying.

He pressed down the accelerator and the Land Rover

shot forward, following the path someone had conveniently made for them.

Shay reached into the back to grab a few extra magazines and grenades to stuff into her tactical vest. Her sword belt lay on the floor in the back seat, but she didn't pick it up.

She gestured to the jungle. "My quick research on the plane indicates a lot of magical creature activity in the deep jungle since the return of magic. The Cambodian government doesn't give a shit if it's not near humans and they've left them alone for the most part, but besides whatever mercenaries we run into, we should be ready for angry and weird shit."

Whispy sent a few excited thoughts that ended with "kill enemies and achieve primary directive," but James did his best to ignore the amulet.

Shay pulled out her phone and tapped a few commands. She frowned. "Tree cover is too thick for satellite comm. That means Peyton and Heather won't be able to back us up."

James shrugged. "We expected that. Don't need babysitters. Besides, if we don't have comm, whoever we run into doesn't either."

"No," Shay replied. "They just don't have sat comm. They could still run drones from line of sight or some shit like that."

"Whatever. I don't even need an EMP for that. I'll just shoot them out of the air."

She laughed. "That might be a fun game."

"Epic fun?"

Shay smirked. "I wouldn't go that far, James." She

looked down at her phone. "Also don't have GPS without the sat link, but the map app shows only a few miles based on estimated time traveled."

James nodded, and a quick mirror and camera check followed before he spoke again. "You think that alien bitch will send another nanoform at me? We might not be in the middle of a fucking blizzard, but we're in the middle of the jungle and can't get decent reception on the satellite phone."

Shay shook her head. "Given the way Heather and Peyton have got shit locked down, I think that alien bitch is in the dark. We didn't have any trouble with Customs or any random mercenaries attacking us."

"What the fuck are you talking about? There's someone already at the site."

She laughed. "Yeah, but I assume those are Durand's buddies. It's not like the alien bitch could have known you would be involved before I took the job, or that you would be involved at all. After all, I do most of my raids by myself or with Lily. It's not like anyone knows Aletheia has Brownstone as backup. Even Erin, who knows all sorts of shit about me, didn't know that." She shrugged. "I think the alien bitch hasn't come after you again because that Wendigo was her best shot and you *still* beat its ass."

"You think the government knows about her? I've been wondering about that ever since Canada."

Shay looked out the window for a moment, two glowing eyes staring at them from a deep, dark stand of trees; a great cat maybe, or something more magical. It didn't matter since seconds later they were hundreds of feet away.

"No, I don't," she replied. "If they knew about her they would know about you, and there's no way they'd leave you alone if they knew that you were an alien. Trust me, Peyton's got a zillion little dark web tripwires looking for that sort of shit. The fact that she went out of her way to have a go at you in an isolated situation only proves it."

The Land Rover bounced hard, passing over a rough patch of terrain.

James grunted. "So just simple mercenary ass-kicking and a treasure hunt?"

Shay laughed. "Yeah, it'll be fun." She looked down at her phone again. "We're now an estimated two miles out. I think we should stop here and hoof it the rest of the way. If assholes are waiting for us, it might help if they couldn't open up on the Rover."

The vehicle coasted to a stop when James eased off the gas. "It's all right if I just kill these fuckers, right? I need to work off my frustration over the Eyes."

Shay nodded. "Yeah. It's not like even if I took Durand alive, I'd get anything out of him." She narrowed her eyes. "And you're too famous, James. We can't let any of these guys see you with me and live."

Whispy continued chattering, anticipation flowing into James' thoughts. Violence made him as happy as playing fetch made Thomas.

James and Shay stepped out of the Land Rover. They didn't bother to pull out the drone in the back but filled their pockets and pouches with all sorts of other useful gear: extra ammo, grenades, several EMPs, and knives. Shay stowed a few magazines containing anti-magic bullets in the top of her tactical vest before slipping on her sword belt.

Although she carried her 9mm in her holster, she'd decided on a Steyr rifle. She slung it over her shoulder.

She pointed to James' coat. "You know what's not epic? That coat. I *swear* there's two of them for every one that gets destroyed. Do you have some sort of artifact producing them?"

"I didn't tell you? I found a wholesaler willing to let me buy them in bulk." James grinned.

Shay sighed. "So there's no chance of me ever getting rid of those damned coats?"

"Not until I find one that has as many pockets." James finished checking his knives and clipped a couple of extra frag grenades to his belt.

Shay rolled her eyes. "Let's go say hello to whoever got here first."

They hiked the last few miles, seeing even fewer signs of wildlife than when they were driving. It was as if the entire jungle knew two apex predators were marching through the trees looking for prey.

James readied his gun at the first sight of angular metal in the distance, but as they closed to a hundred yards and spotted six green trucks but no people, he frowned. A natural clearing served as a parking lot for the vehicles.

A crumbled stone structure covered by vines was visible about fifty yards past the trucks, trees obscuring much of its detail.

"You see anyone?" he asked.

Shay lowered her AR goggles and tapped the side. She snickered.

"Yeah, we've got a half-dozen thermal signatures lying down on each side in the main tree line. All humanoid. Running a little hot, too." Shay tapped the goggles again. "I'm almost insulted they thought it would be that easy." She shook her head. "These guys must not be with Durand. Too sloppy."

"Not like he knew you were coming." James shrugged.

Shay pulled the rifle off her shoulder and flipped the safety off. "How about I take the guys on the right and you take the guys on the left?" She gestured to the golden nimbus that still surrounded her. "Doubt they are using anti-magic bullets, so this should be a nice warmup."

James grunted and readied his .45. "Just gonna shoot first and ask questions later."

"Fine by me. Three...two...one."

They sprinted to either side of the clearing. The vehicles were all parked in the center, James presumed by design, since trying to take cover by them would leave him open to attacks from his flanks.

He'd cleared about ten yards when the loud crack of rifles broke the still of the clearing. Muzzle flashes announced the position of the enemy and their bullets slammed into James, stinging but not doing much else.

Kill the enemy, Whispy demanded. *Minimal adaptation potential.*

The men on the other side opened up on Shay. A charging woman with a long sword on her hip and literally glowing was probably the easiest and most obvious target of their careers. Her golden field flashed as their bullets struck, but she didn't slow.

Shay brought her Steyr down and fired a burst into the brush concealing the men. A man screamed. The men on both sides popped up, revealing they were all in ghillie suits.

Guess that explains why they looked hot to Shay. Lot of effort to set up an ambush. Almost feel sorry for the assholes, except for the fact that they are trying to ambush us.

Inefficient optical camouflage, Whispy responded.

What, can you turn me invisible?

High power required, Whispy responded. *Inefficient power to tactical utility. Power insufficient for extended advanced transformation.*

Doesn't matter. Don't need that shit yet, but I'll keep it in mind.

James' opponents kept up their fire and bullet after bullet bounced off him. He didn't fire yet, seeing no point in wasting bullets until he was closer.

A man to his right screamed, Shay's bullets finding their mark. The men rushed into the tree line, seeking cover, their attacks doing nothing against their enhanced foes.

James yanked a grenade off his belt, pulled the pin, and tossed it toward the men, the deadly explosive hurtling through the air. A couple of the men tried to leap out of the way, but the explosion shredded them. They didn't even have a chance to scream before they died.

The four remaining men on James' side also rushed for the trees. Their dark makeup concealed their faces at this distance, but he imagined they were regretting coming to Cambodia.

Too fucking bad. You made an unfortunate career choice, assholes.

James grinned and holstered his pistol as the men kept up their barrages. He pulled out a Ka-Bar and charged toward the closest man.

The man didn't run or flinch. He pointed his rifle right at James' head and fired a burst. The bullets bounced off with a slight sting as James closed the distance and slammed his knife into the man's eye.

He yanked it out, blood spurting all over his coat and face before he sheathed it and grabbed the man's rifle. Two of the remaining men kept up their fire. Another dropped his rifle and yanked out a stun rod.

James ignored the last man and rushed toward one of the men pelting him with bullets. When he slammed the rifle into the enemy's head, the stock cracked, and judging by the indent, the man's skull did as well.

The stun rod man gritted his teeth and backed up, but his final comrade turned and ran. James whipped out a throwing knife and flung it into the back of his head.

With a grunt, James turned to face the final enemy on his side. He spared a quick glance for Shay. She was watching from a distance, and no more gunshots rang out from her side.

Took 'em already, huh? Don't worry, this shit won't take long.

Whispy radiated annoyance.

Kill all enemies. Proceed to new enemies to maximize adaptation.

James wiped blood off his face. "Do you know who I am? What's your deal—tomb raider or mercenary?"

"I like to think of myself as a private military contractor

first, shitbag." The other man raised his stun rod. "You shouldn't have gotten close. Every man has a weakness, and this isn't a normal stun rod."

James gestured for the man to attack him. "Let's see if you found mine then, asshole."

The mercenary charged James with a yell and jammed the stun rod against his neck with a huge grin on his face. The rod crackled as it discharged into James.

"Tickles," the bounty hunter replied. He grabbed the man's hand and squeezed, the bones cracking under the pressure.

The mercenary screamed.

James grabbed him by the throat and lifted him. "I had a shitty day yesterday. Might have been feeling more merciful otherwise." He smashed the man's head into the tree and dropped the body to the forest floor. "Then again, you tried to kill me, so probably not, asshole."

He snorted and marched toward the still-glowing Shay.

Shay shouldered her rifle and shrugged. "None of those guys were Durand." She walked over to one of the men James had dispatched and frowned down at his body. "Yeah, probably not his guys even." She moved on to the next body.

After a few moments, she finished examining the bodies and frowned.

"No Durand?" James asked.

Shay nodded. "Whoever these guys were, they didn't know we were coming, or they would have brought better equipment. I thought they'd at least slap in some anti-magic bullets or something." She shook her head.

"Not everyone can be a badass." James shrugged.

"Fuckers should have given up. Wasn't like I was gonna chase their asses through the jungle."

"Five points for bravery, not that it'll help them now that they're all dead." Shay snorted.

James glanced at the parked trucks and frowned. "Too many trucks for too few guys."

Shay nodded. "I noticed. Maybe these guys really hate carpooling." She gestured to the crumbling stone in the distance. "I'm guessing the rest are already inside. Not sure if they have comms with them or not, but they might have heard the gunfire."

"Good," James rumbled. "That'll make them come out quicker then. No reason for this shit to take forever. I've still got an appointment with the Eyes back in LA."

CHAPTER TWELVE

Kathy smiled down at the bar. She'd polished the wood so well she could see her own reflection in it. She patted her hair.

Damn. I look good. Nothing wrong with looking good and being smart at the same time.

She grinned. Even if things were proceeding slower on the opening of the White Sun than she would have preferred, she wanted to take the time to get things right. Tyler might be her partner, but he wasn't her boss, which meant she could have a different aesthetic than the Black Sun—which managed to still look dingy despite the money poured into the remodel. A nice TV didn't make a place classy.

It's like Tyler's allergic to anything not dark. Jeez, a few earth tones wouldn't kill you.

Her phone rang and she whipped it out of her pocket, eager for news. She'd been expecting a call from one of the contractors in Vegas to go over choices for the restroom.

Tyler didn't understand that a good restroom layout could do a lot for a place.

Kathy frowned as she looked at the phone. Not the contractor, unless he'd switched phones. Unknown number, not rare in the info broker business, but not something she wanted or needed at that moment.

Kathy brought the phone to her face. "Hello?"

Someone wheezed over the line and her heart stomach tightened.

Oh, shit. Please not him. It's been months. Why does he have to fucking bother me now?

"It's so lovely to talk to you again, Kathy," rasped the Eyes.

She sighed and ran a hand through her hair. "I wish I could say the same."

"It's appropriate that you feel that way." He let out a cold, hollow laugh. "Healthy fear leads to people living longer than pointless and arrogant bravery."

"Duly noted. What's this about?" Kathy did her best to keep her fear out of her voice. The last thing she wanted was for the weird bastard to know he still haunted her dreams. The line between healthy fear and lasting terror was pretty thin when it came to the Eyes.

"You haven't come to me for some time." the Eyes replied. "I'm disappointed. I hoped you would have more reason to come and talk to me, especially now that you're going to run off to Vegas and play at independence. I know things. I know people there. You'll find me still useful, or at least the information I can provide to those willing to pay the price."

Kathy snorted. "Yeah, because I'm going to drive back

to LA every time I need a tidbit. No, thanks. I think I'll cultivate local contacts."

The Eyes offered her a cold laugh. "No matter. It doesn't change the fact that you still owe me for past services rendered, little girl."

The woman took a deep breath to steady her voice. "I'm aware of that, but you weren't clear on what I owe you."

"That's not true. I've been very clear about what you owe me. You owe me an answer."

"Yeah, but an answer to what question?" Kathy frowned. "It's not like you'll take the answer to why did the chicken cross the road."

"Come to me now, and you'll learn what I need from you." A quiet wheeze sounded over the line. "Or run now and keep running forever, because you'll always have to look over your shoulder. Vegas won't be far enough. Even Oriceran won't be far enough. There's nowhere you can run that I won't be able to find you." The Eyes wheezed mocking laughter. "If you find that too cryptic, then let me be clear this one time. You will come to me now, or you'll suffer for not paying your existing debts."

Kathy swallowed and sighed. "Fine. I'm on my way."

"Good." He ended the call.

Kathy lowered the phone and stared at it with a frown, then marched into the hallway and headed toward Tyler's office. She pounded on his door.

"What the fuck?" he yelled from inside. "There better be someone dead out there, and if there is, let the fucking cops handle it. I'm trying to read through a bunch of shit."

Kathy threw open the door. "I've got to go."

Tyler frowned at her from behind his desk. "In the middle of your shift?"

"Yeah. The Eyes made that real damned clear." Kathy shrugged. "If you don't see me by tomorrow, the Eyes killed me. I'd tell you to avenge my death, but there's no money in it for you, so at least write a mean anonymous comment about him online."

Tyler snorted. "Don't be so dramatic. He isn't going to kill you."

"Why are you so sure of that?" Kathy crossed her arms. "I don't think that guy has any sort of restraint other than he doesn't want to push too far until the AET kicks in his door."

"I'm sure because he might be a sick fuck from some evil demon land in Oriceran or whatever, but he's a lot like me in one important way." Tyler smirked.

Kathy blinked. "What the hell? How are you like the Eyes?"

Tyler shrugged. "We both know that you don't throw away a useful tool. Just make sure that the Eyes still sees you as a useful tool and you'll walk out of there still breathing, maybe just a little more freaked out for your time." A dark expression covered his face. "I'm serious. Make sure he sees you as a useful tool no matter what it takes, Kathy."

"Fine. I will." She looked away and nodded. "I'll be glad when I move to Vegas."

Kathy took a deep breath as she stepped in front of the doors to the Eyes' office, if it was even appropriate to call an empty room an office.

Too bad I don't have any bombs sitting around my apartment.

Two scowling elves in suits guarded the room. They stared at Kathy with disgust in their eyes.

I don't have time for your bullshit, assholes.

Kathy nodded toward the double doors. "I get that you think I'm a roach, but the Eyes personally called me here. Trust me, I wouldn't be here if I had another choice."

One of the elves smirked and nodded. He pulled open the doors and gestured her inside. Unlike the last time she'd visited, there were no light sources in the room. The dim light from the hallway illuminated the front half, revealing scored and bloodstained tile on the floor.

"Oh, you've got to be fucking kidding me," Kathy muttered. She sighed and clutched her purse tighter. Her gun might help, although she didn't have anti-magic bullets, so she doubted it. If the Eyes were that easy to kill, someone would have taken him out a long time ago.

She stepped inside and the elf closed the doors behind her, plunging her into complete darkness. There wasn't even any light coming from beneath the door. Her heart beat harder, and she took a few deep breaths.

It wasn't the dark that was frightening; it was what might be hiding in it. Maybe twenty years ago people could lie and say no monsters lurked in the shadows, but the return of magic had changed that forever.

"Okay, you summoned me, oh Great Lord of Information," Kathy offered, her tone infused with all the defiant sarcasm she could muster despite her pounding heart. "And I've come to give you the answer I owe you. Just let me know how I can do that."

The air around her turned frigid. She rubbed her shoulders to warm them and blew out a breath, her expelled breath visible as a fine mist.

"So strong of will," the Eyes whispered into her ear from behind her. "I've done experiments with so many strong-willed humans. The results are always interesting. Everyone breaks in the end, you know. Your species is weak. That's why you scurry around, so desperate to accomplish something in your short, pathetic lives."

Kathy's teeth chattered. The cold sensation she'd encountered before when dealing with the Eyes had been nowhere near as intense as her current experience.

"If you want an answer about what I think about humans compared to every random race on Oriceran, I don't know what to tell you," she replied. "I don't even know all the races on Oriceran. Elves and gnomes are weird enough for me to wrap my mind around, let alone things like you. If you want me to admit you could break me, then fine—I admit that. I'm not a soldier or a bounty hunter, and I agree, humans don't live a long time. It's not like you're saying anything humans haven't been saying for all of our history."

Fucking asshole. You hide here, but someday you're going to push the wrong person, and they'll end you.

Yellow eyes glowed on the opposite side of the room.

"Bounty hunter?" rasped the Eyes, something approaching annoyance in his voice. "Why did you choose that as an example of bravery and strength of will? They are parasites, in a sense. Loyal to no one and nothing but money."

"Maybe." Kathy shrugged. "It takes a lot of balls to go after dangerous criminals, and I don't know him well, but it's hard to think of someone more impressive than James Brownstone." She smiled, a little confidence filtering back into her. "I get that he uses artifacts, but he's still human. I wonder if you could break him so eas—"

The yellow eyes disappeared, and darkness retook the room. A deep, penetrating cold attacked her wrist, agony shooting through her arm. She fell to her knees and screamed. A few seconds later, the pain stopped.

Kathy panted and ran her fingers over her wrist. She didn't feel anything wrong. Her skin was cold, but there was no sign of frostbite and no further pain.

What the fuck was that? Is he getting into my head?

"Brownstone is just a man," wheezed the Eyes, seemingly from all around Kathy. "A man who has let his arrogance blind him to his natural limits. I was content to leave him be as he did me, but he has gone too far. He has forgotten his place."

"Meaning what?" Kathy replied, her voice barely above a whisper. "You think you're going to take on James Brownstone?" She shook her head. "Do you ever watch the news? You might be tough, but he's tougher."

"Enough. It's time for your answer, Kathy." The Eyes laughed, the sound mocking and containing not a hint of actual mirth. "You'll repay your debt by answering a simple question: do you value *your* life more than others?"

Kathy scrambled to her feet. "I...of course I do. I'm a

survivor. It's why I left New York. It's why I'm still breathing."

"Your lies are transparent, little girl, and I see right through you. You'll leave this place. In your car, you'll find a small golden orb. You will take this orb and place it in James Brownstone's house within the next forty-eight hours, or you will die painfully and slowly as part of my next experiment."

"I…you…" Kathy sputtered. Her breaths turned ragged as her heart threatened to explode out of her chest.

"What?" the Eyes rasped. "You want to say, 'I can't do this?' or 'I won't do this?' But you already answered me, Kathy. You value your life more than others, and it's not as if you owe anything to James Brownstone. He gave you some money and a little pat on the head because you helped him. Nothing more. You will help me, and then you will be free from me."

Somehow I doubt that, freak.

Kathy looked down, unsure what to say.

I'll just stall. He's talking about Brownstone being arrogant, but the Eyes is ridiculous. If Brownstone doesn't come back soon, I can just go to the police. Even if I die, they can probably get some wizard to prove that the spell came from the Eyes. At least the bastard will go down.

Kathy lifted her head, a defiant glare on her face although she wasn't sure if he could tell in the darkness.

"I know what you're thinking, little girl," the Eyes murmured. "You're thinking you'll tell Brownstone or the police and watch as the AET raid my club. Laugh at my presumption. Go ahead and try to tell someone. The pain you felt before was a powerful curse. You won't be able to tell anyone what I've asked you to do. If you do tell them, you will die." He chuckled. "And this way I'll learn if your answer matches your actions. Another interesting experiment. Humans are pathetic but interesting."

Damn it. He isn't as arrogant as I needed. I'm so screwed. Okay, calm down. Need to think this through. All puzzles can be solved. First step is just getting the information I need.

"What's the orb do?" Kathy asked.

"You don't need to know. Just know you have forty-eight hours to place it in Brownstone's home. Not on, *in*. Now leave, and don't you dare come back until you've placed the orb. I'll know if you fail me."

The doors squeaked open, and light poured into the room. Kathy backed out slowly, blinking, and bile rose in the back of her throat.

The elves closed the door behind her, hateful smirks on their faces.

Fuck you, assholes. One day your boss is going to experiment on you, I bet, and then you'll be sorry.

Kathy stumbled down the hall to the front door. She blinked and stopped as she realized that something was peeking out from under her sleeve on the arm where she'd felt the pain.

She rolled back her sleeve. An intricate series of rounded glyphs marked her arm. Each was a different color, but they didn't move or glow. If she'd woken up in the middle of the night and seen them, she'd think they were nothing more than tattoos.

"Oh, shit," she whispered.

An hour later, Kathy knocked on a nondescript door on the second floor of a run-down apartment building in Elf Town.

"Come on," she whispered. "You have to be here. I don't have time for you not to be here."

Kathy pulled her phone out of her pocket and stared down at the timer she'd set. She hadn't even bothered telling Tyler anything after leaving the Eyes' place other than she was taking the next couple of days off. Fortunately, he hadn't pressed her for a reason, but he, more than anyone else she knew, understood what it was like dealing with the yellow-eyed bastard.

She knocked on the door again and took a deep breath.

Will this trigger the curse? A lot of the crap I've read said those things are usually specific. Damn it. I can't do nothing. There's no guarantee the Eyes won't kill me even if I deliver the damned orb.

The door swung open to reveal an amused-looking elf in dark blue silk pajamas. "Can I help you?" He looked her up and down. "Tyler didn't contact me about you coming over."

"Yeah, sorry to bother you, Dannec, but I'll offer you ten thousand dollars right now, no questions, no explanations, if you'll check me for magic," Kathy spat. "This has nothing to do with Tyler."

The elf raised an eyebrow and clucked his tongue. "Desperation is a horrible thing to bring to any business transaction. Tyler understands this, but you obviously still need to learn."

Kathy shrugged, keeping her face nonchalant even as

her heart thundered. "You want the money or not? I don't have a lot of time to fuck around tonight."

"Easy money isn't something I turn away." Dannec gestured inside. "Payment up front." He held up his hand, and an account address appeared in glowing green letters above his palm. "Send this amount in TrollCoin to that address."

The woman nodded and entered his apartment. She pulled out her phone and initiated the transfer. She was used to paying for illicit deals with different cryptocurrencies.

The elf's phone buzzed from his coffee table, and he smiled.

Kathy blinked as she finally took in the apartment. Two huge tables filled the living room. Several massive bones, each easily over six feet long, sat on the tables.

"What the hell are…" She shook her head. "Know what? Never mind. Sometimes it's best not to know."

Dannec grinned. "Now you're learning." He rubbed his hands together. "So, you want to know what magic is on you, hmm? I should tell you for the future that there are far cheaper ways to go about finding that sort of thing out, but I'll enjoy your money."

"Sometimes convenience is worth the premium." Kathy shrugged.

"Care to tell me why you want to know?"

"No." Kathy shook her head. "Not at all."

Dannec nodded. "Fair enough, and not strictly necessary. To be clear, the money you paid only covers me examining you. If I find something unpleasant, which I'm guessing I will, it'll cost you a lot more to get rid of it, and I offer no guarantees that I'll even be able to do that."

"That's my problem. "

"Also true. I applaud your clear thinking on this matter." Dannec chuckled.

The elf raised his hands and half-closed his eyes. He murmured, but a clear and sharp melody filled the air as a glow surrounded his hands. After a moment, he lowered his hands.

He clucked his tongue. "Kathy, what did you do to end up with that powerful of a curse on you? Not to be rude, but you're simply not important enough to warrant the kind of magic that's been expended on you. And before you ask, neither is Tyler."

Kathy shrugged and let out a pained snort. "What can I say? Somedays are just kind of crappy. Can you remove it?"

Dannec burst out laughing, and her heart sank.

He shook his head. "Even if I were an expert on bizarre and powerful curses, which I'm not, trying to remove it would probably kill us both, but I'm always willing to make money. I can look into it and ask around for a price, but unfortunately, because of the nature of the magic, I'll have to charge you a premium. It's extremely dark and danger-ous, the kind of thing that might attract the wrong sort of attention from both Oriceran and Earth authorities if they think I'm dabbling in it. Besides, I suspect it'd take a team of magic users to remove that curse from you, or someone of extraordinary power."

What the hell? Just what is *the Eyes?*

Kathy sighed and shook her head. "Don't bother. The problem's going to be solved one way or another soon enough, and I'd rather keep my money in case I somehow win my gamble."

"Your gamble?"

She shook her head. "Don't ask. I'm not going to say anything more."

"Fair enough, but you're sure?"

Kathy nodded. "Yes. I've got decisions to make soon."

Dannec furrowed his brow. "You obviously came knowing there was magic on you, so I don't understand why you don't want me to look into it for you. Why did you come here, then?"

Kathy stepped out the front door and looked over her shoulder. "Because I needed to make sure before I did something very stupid that someone wasn't bluffing. Thanks, Dannec. I appreciate it. Buy something cool with my money."

"If you change your mind, give me a call." Dannec offered her a slight smile. "And welcome to the world of dangerous magic."

Kathy waved and headed toward the stairs. The visit might have been expensive, but it hadn't been pointless. She now knew the curse was real, and more importantly, she knew the curse wasn't all-encompassing. Asking Dannec to check her out hadn't killed her.

You left me a hole, Eyes. Now this is just another puzzle for me to solve, except this time it's my life on the line. Great motivation.

Kathy snorted. "I'm not going to lose to some freak. I'll show him that humans are more resourceful than he thinks."

CHAPTER THIRTEEN

James and Shay half-expected more mercenaries to pop out when they approached the ruins, but no one else showed up. No snipers fired from the trees as they closed on the entrance.

A partially-collapsed archway led into a sloping stone tunnel in the ground. Piles of rock and overgrown weeds covered half the entrance.

Shay crouched nearby and pointed to a boot print. "So they *did* go inside. I'm guessing a dozen guys, maybe two dozen near the top range, based on the vehicles and the guys we already killed."

James shrugged. "Don't really give a shit. If they don't have better weapons, we'll beat their asses easily."

"I agree." Shay stood, a slight frown on her face. "I'm wondering if this is some merc company that decided to try their hand at tomb raiding. Too damned sloppy for pro tomb raiders. Even Hollingsworth would be smarter than this."

"That's a good thing. Means they'll be less annoying."

Shay nodded. "Maybe. I'm worried about idiots waking something up."

Whispy perked up at that.

Engage stronger unknown enemies for maximum adaptation.

James furrowed his brow. "Might be fun."

"You know what, you're right!" Shay laughed. "You see? We can have a good time on his-and-hers ass-kicking trips. Just have to keep it warm."

She lowered her AR goggles and tapped the side. "Going to stick with normal vision mode for now. Hard to use low-light mode when I'm glowing anyway." She strapped on a headlamp and a wrist light.

"Sounds good." James followed her lead.

Shay patted her rifle and smiled as she stepped toward the entrance. "If there are a bunch of assholes in there, they might save us some time by taking care of traps and any weird creatures lying around."

She stepped into the cave, the soft glow of her shield aura combined with her lights to push back the darkness.

Although the ceiling had collapsed in several places, depositing mounds of dirt and stone, the rectangular tunnel extended down at a shallow angle for dozens of yards before angling to the side. They proceeded down it.

After a couple of minutes of walking, Shay chuckled.

"What?" James asked. "See someone?"

"No, not yet. I was laughing about something else. You ever think about how we met?"

He shrugged. "Through the Professor. What about it?"

"That first job in Peru." Shay smiled. "I was looking for that artifact, and you were there to help handle the Red Warlocks. I thought you were a lot of talk at first. I even hated that you were coming, but then you took those guys out like they were grade-schoolers."

James grunted. "They got cocky. It cost them."

Shay laughed. "It impressed me, and at that time not a lot was impressing me. For a while, though, I didn't want to work with you even when the Professor suggested it. I got pissed at the mere mention of it."

He frowned and looked her way. "Why? Back then I was only interested in bounties, not taking a cut of your artifact money."

"I didn't like the idea of having to depend on you." Shay shrugged. "I was still figuring out what it meant to be a tomb raider. It wasn't just you. I didn't want to depend on anyone. It took me a while to start trusting Peyton, and I had something to hold over his head, at least. You, though…"

James chuckled. "Yeah, I get taking a long time to learn to depend on others."

"And I was annoyed that you weren't coming onto me, too."

He groaned. "Not that shit again."

Shay smirked. "I figured it out eventually, and you're one to talk. You thought I was a stripper or some shit."

James shrugged. "Mistakes happen."

Whispy remained quiet in James' mind, his only contribution a vague projection of anticipation.

You're as bad as Thomas when I get his leash, James thought at the amulet.

Shay stopped and threw up a hand. James pulled his gun and she unslung her rifle and crept forward, her brow furrowed.

Someone lay unmoving behind a pile of collapsed stone from the ceiling. The pair approached, their weapons trained on the target, but whoever it was didn't move or even twitch.

Shay tapped the side of her goggles a few times. "Oh, that explains it." She tapped her goggles again and jogged toward the person. James frowned and followed.

A man in a khaki uniform lay on the ground, impaled through the neck by a dark-blue crystal. His eyes were open, and a rifle rested between his legs.

James stared down at the man's chest. "What the fuck is that crystal? Some sort of monster?"

Shay shook her head and pointed toward the wall and a small diamond-shaped hole. "Trap, I'm thinking. Though might be partially magical because of the crystal." She shrugged and stood. "A merc took a hit for us, just like I was hoping, but we can't get complacent. Once they lost a guy or two to the traps, I'm sure they started being more careful."

She activated the thermal mode on her goggles and stared down the hallway. "Okay, that's weird."

"What?" James peered into the darkness but saw only more stone and dirt.

Shay pointed back the way they came. "Faint thermal trail to this point for the whole way, along with some fresher stuff that marks us, and barely-there signals that I'm guessing came from a large group." She gestured deeper into the hallway. "But nothing past this point. It's like this guy got killed, and they turned and ran." She shined her light on the ground. "Not seeing any footprints, though."

James shrugged. "Maybe they did run. They might be badass mercenaries when it comes to shooting up relief caravans or shit like that, but if they don't do tomb raids, they might have been chickenshit about traps."

"You're saying the entire group was out there then?" Shay pursed her lips. "Doesn't feel right."

"Yeah, I agree. You sure there isn't a second location?"

Shay looked at him. "A second location?"

James nodded. "More ruins, a different spot where the lance might be."

"There could be, but not that I know of based on the information I have." She frowned. "Still, that might explain it. No way to follow a decent thermal trail outside though because of how warm it is. That might mean we finish this off and come out to another pack of mercenaries."

"Kind of like dessert." James smiled.

Shay grinned. "You're really enjoying yourself, aren't you? Not that I'm complaining, it's a big difference between this and Canada."

James nodded. "The Council was a big deal, and we paid a big price for it." He looked down for a moment.

I made them pay, Shorty. I made all the fuckers pay.

He looked back up. "He Who Hunts went after a bunch of people in an amusement park, and the nanite shit was just annoying." He grunted. "But this is straight ass-kicking. I don't have to worry about anyone getting hurt who doesn't have it coming, and even if I don't kill every last motherfucker we run into, I don't think they'll end up in LA turning people into monsters underground."

"Good point." Shay started back down the hallway, her pace slower than before. "It'll be nice to get the huge payday after this, but it'll also be hard getting used to lower-paying jobs afterward." She laughed. "Maybe Aletheia should stop getting out of bed for less than forty million dollars."

James followed Shay, his larger strides making it easy to catch up. "Could start a tomb raiding agency. Kind of like those Hollingsworth guys. Carson Retrieval Specialists or the Carson Team."

"Some of us are meant for that kind of thing, and some of us are meant to stay under the radar." She snickered. "Helping train Lily is more than enough for me. Unless Alison wants to take up tomb raiding, although the few times I've asked her, she didn't seem that interested."

"Huh. Good point." James rubbed his chin. "She's halfway through her second year of school now. Graduation's just a couple years off. Got to think about the future."

Shay nodded. "Sure, she can do the bounty hunting with you for a while, but it might be nice for her to have a touch of normalcy. Go to a normal college for a few years."

James grunted. "Like UCLA?"

"Sure, why not?" Shay frowned and froze. She tapped the other side of her goggles and pointed at the wall. "Another trap in there."

He stepped in front of her. "Maybe I should just trip it and get it over with."

"Huh? What the hell are you thinking, James?"

He patted his chest. "I've got potions, and if there's gonna be a lot of fucking traps, might help to get Whispy trained on whatever the fuck they have."

The amulet's excitement filled James' mind.

Achieve additional adaptation. Achieve primary directive.

Shay took a deep breath and nodded. She reached into a pouch and pulled out one of James' healing potions. "Based on what we saw on the other guy, it'll activate when you walk past the line. I'm not seeing any sort of trigger, so I'm guessing it's magical."

James walked forward, his gaze fixed on the wall. It flashed and hissed, and a glowing crystal shot out. He spun to take the hit on his left arm.

He hissed as the projectile embedded itself and pain blasted through his limb.

Yes, Whispy hissed in his mind. *Adaptation in progress.*

James reached up and yanked the now blood-soaked crystal out with a grunt. He gritted his teeth. "Yeah, that fucking hurt a little, but it didn't end me."

Shay offered him the potion. "Sometimes I wonder if you're secretly a masochist."

He looked down at his throbbing arm.

Can you heal that shit?

Regeneration in process, Whispy replied.

James waved off the potion. "It'll be fine." He rotated the arm. The ache was already slightly less. "A scratch."

"You're sure?" Shay stared at his arm, concern on her face. "Doesn't look like a scratch to me."

"Yeah." James lowered his arm. Best he could tell it'd already stopped bleeding. "Doesn't stop me from being annoyed with the fucking ancient Cambodians, even if I took the shot on purpose."

Shay shook her head. "Magical crystal traps aren't very Khmer. One thing I've learned by studying revised history is that even if a lot of legends and myths aren't a hundred percent accurate, they are decent proxies for the types of magic associated with those cultures throughout their history." She pointed to the crystal on the ground. "And nothing about that screams Khmer Empire era. Probably Oricerans.

"Given that we're looking for an Atlantean crystal lance, I don't think it's a coincidence that magic crystals are shooting out. Probably old-school Atlantean magic. They took over this place, or maybe convinced the locals they were gods or something. Doesn't matter. They obviously aren't here anymore."

High adaptation potential, Whispy noted.

Yeah, not like I run into a lot of Atlanteans, though. Don't know how useful this shit will be, now that I think about it.

Maximum adaptation necessary for primary directive.

Whatever the fuck that *is.*

James chuckled. "If there's gonna be a lot of this shit, I should just march out in front and take all the hits."

Shay furrowed her brow. "It was one thing when we were in Warehouse Three training your amulet. I was careful."

"You shot me, shocked me, and threw grenades at me."

She shrugged. "I made sure not to shoot you in the head, though."

"Who knows? Might even be able to come back from that." James smiled.

She rolled her eyes. "We don't know that, and I don't want to try it."

"I've been shot in the head before and survived." He patted the side of his head.

"But you haven't taken brain damage. I don't want to

have to get to know you again. The first time was fucking exhausting enough."

James considered that for a few seconds before nodding. "Good point. Just keep pointing out traps, and I'll try to take the hit in the arm or chest. If it's the same kind of trap, it won't matter. I'm already partially adapted to that shit. Next time, I bet it won't do more than scratch me."

Shay nodded. "Okay. I'll admit it's not a bad idea to train Whispy more on this shit, especially if we run into some weird Atlantean security guard later on." She motioned forward. "But let's move slow and steady. Not like we're in a hurry. Even if Durand showed up, he obviously didn't go farther in." She shrugged. "For now, it looks like we're in the lead in this race. Let's go find ourselves a forty-million-dollar lance!"

CHAPTER FOURTEEN

Five more minutes brought them to a T-junction. James' wound had sealed itself by the time they arrived.

Shay used her AR goggles to scan the area. "It could be either way. Nothing unusual I can detect in any of the different modes. I figure we go right, then come back left. Just be systematic." She pointed at him. "Since you're with me, we shouldn't need to worry about mapping or marking my path. That memory is convenient for tomb raids."

James nodded.

They proceeded down the hallway. Although the roof became noticeably lower, the stone hallways were smooth and covered with dust, but still intact. Shay located additional traps along the way.

The second one only gave James a minor cut and the third, a scratch.

The hallway split off again at another junction, several open chambers lining the corridors on either side. They took the right fork again.

James and Shay entered the first chamber and looked around. A few shattered pieces of pottery lay on the ground, but there was nothing else of interest.

"Do you think there used to be a lot of shit in here and people stole it?" he asked. "I mean, like old-school tomb raiders, kind of how like ancient thieves stole so much shit from the Pyramids."

Shay shrugged. "Maybe. Thieves alive closer to the time this place was built might have known more about the kind of magic and traps in here and could avoid them, or maybe the entire complex was abandoned one day." She knelt and eyed some of the pottery shards. "It's times like this that tomb raiding gets a little closer to real archaeology. Slow and steady while we look for the big find."

A thud echoed through the halls.

James spun toward the doorway, his gun at the ready.

Shay unslung her rifle and frowned. "Maybe the second-place crew decided to finally catch up. I was hoping if they were out there, they wouldn't be so brave."

Another thud echoed. It sounded like the noise was coming from farther down the hallway.

"Or they were ahead of us the entire time," James muttered. He nodded toward the door. "Might as well clean this shit up, so the fuckers aren't biting our asses later."

"Agreed."

They jogged into the hallway, weapons at the ready. They didn't hear any more thuds, but near-constant scratching emanated from deeper in the darkness.

"Doesn't sound like mercs," James rumbled. "Sounds like an animal, maybe."

Shay nodded. "Maybe some of those local creatures the government's letting run free."

Engage and kill new enemies, Whispy ordered. *Moderate adaptation potential.*

Way ahead of you, Coach.

James waited for the inevitable rebuke from the amulet, but it didn't come. He grinned.

Getting used to it there, huh, Coach Whispy Doom?

Importance of tactical efficiency exceeds all other considerations.

James snorted. *Figure it's easier than bitching at me, huh?*

Link error acknowledged.

The bounty hunter decided to let it drop. The amulet had complained about link errors before, but he would never give a clear answer on what that meant. As long as Whispy was providing defense against the upcoming enemy, that would be enough.

The scratching grew louder as Shay and James headed down the hall, passing several rooms, most empty but a few with rubble. A long stone table flanked by two stone benches covered in a thick layer of dark dust was the first interesting sight in any of the rooms.

As Shay and James ventured farther down the dark hall, there were no more doors on the sides. Their lights revealed a wide opening to a much larger chamber at the end, though. Several barbed-tentacled forms slithered in the distance, the beams from their headlamps and wrist lights reflecting off angular crystalline surfaces.

"Yeah, definitely not mercs." James grunted. "Unless they're weird-ass Oricerans who took a wrong turn."

Shay grinned. "Travel the world, see new things, meet new people, kill new creatures. I love my life."

James chuckled and nodded as he jogged ahead. "Not gonna try to get hit, but maybe all those traps were the same kind of magic those things use."

"Here's hoping." Shay advanced behind him.

They reached the opening to the chamber, which gave them a better view of their foes. A mass of white crystalline slender-bodied creatures slithered over the floor, each over four feet in length. Glowing blue circles, possibly eyes, covered most of their bodies, and seven tentacles were attached to each creature. Some tentacles trailed behind them, but most of the beasts were using three or four to crawl.

Piles of the dull, cracked bodies of the creatures covered the ground several deep. None of the corpses displayed any of the glowing circles, and most were missing tentacles. The room must have contained hundreds of bodies and dozens of their active brethren.

James nodded toward the piles. "Think those are dead or just asleep?"

"Not a cryptozoologist, but I'm guessing those are dead." Shay laughed. "Hope so, or this is gonna be an interesting next few minutes."

James grunted. "I've fought worse."

Whispy urged him to battle.

"Not sure how tough they are yet." Shay shrugged. "Crystal squids. That's different, even for me."

James frowned. "They only have seven tentacles, though. That's not the right number for a squid."

Shay snorted. "It's easier to call them crystal squids than make something new up."

"Good point. Wonder if they're nanoforms?" He narrowed his eyes.

Can you tell, Whispy?

Direct sampling required to verify. Engage and kill enemy.

Shay tapped her AR goggles a few times, her lips pursed. "Thermal readings match the background, but getting something interesting in the UV range—all sorts of different patterns." She shrugged. "Not that I know what a nanoform should look like in different spectra."

"The Wendigo blended in heat-wise, too. Maybe that means something." James kept his gun trained on the nearest squid. "Or maybe it means shit."

A couple more squids wriggled out of a hole in the corner of the roof. James focused his light there. The squids didn't react, but he frowned.

"The hole is round," he declared.

Shay shrugged. "So? That's not a stunning rarity in the world of holes."

He shook his head. "Perfectly round. I think it was created on purpose—like artificially by the Atlanteans or the humans, not the squids."

"No doors in this place…you notice that?" Shay muttered. "If these things were here to begin with, whoever was here, human or otherwise, had to have a way to control them. Maybe that's why they're not attacking. Maybe they need some sort of activation code or spell."

Three more emerged from a hole on the opposite side of the room.

Kill the enemy, Whispy chanted. *Kill the enemy.*

Doesn't seem like they are the enemy. Not gonna fuck up someone's pets just because they aren't around. You've seen what I do to people who hurt my *pets.*

James shrugged. "Might as well get out of here. They aren't attacking."

"Yeah." Shay shrugged. "If they're just going to sit here and have a squid party, might as well leave them alone."

They backed out of the room and returned to the hall. The scuttling intensified, but after a few seconds it stopped entirely, an eerie silence descending over the chamber.

Glowing blue patterns played across the creatures' skin.

"What the fuck are they doing?" James raised his gun.

A harsh, dissonant cry rose from all the monsters at once, but they remained stationary.

"Hell if I know." Shay frowned. "I'm guessing it's not gonna be good for us."

Another cry sounded from the squids.

Kill the enemy, Whispy demanded.

Shay sighed and slapped a hand to her forehead. "Of course. It's not like they had computers and networking back then."

James grunted. "Meaning what?"

She raised her rifle. "I'm guessing they're waiting for some sort of command phrase."

James grunted. "Like what?"

"See any seven-hundred-year-old Cambodians or Atlanteans around to ask?" Shay shrugged. "For all we know it could be, 'Kiss my ass.'"

Three staccato cries erupted from the squids, and they surged forward.

"Looks like Whispy's gonna get what he wanted," James muttered.

He opened fire, and Shay joined him. The first few squids twitched and rolled to a halt, blue fluid leaking from the bullet wounds. James wasn't sure if it was blood, but it was easier to think of it that way.

Whispy's excitement died down as the pair continued taking the creatures out. Soon a pile of motionless crystal squids lay in front of them.

Not enough for you, Whispy?

Minimum adaptation potential.

Shay switched to burst fire and emptied her magazine. Some of the squids climbed the walls and ceiling, forming a writhing mass of crystalline tentacles crawling toward James and Shay. Other monsters charged through their fallen brethren as she reloaded, knocking the bodies aside without apparent concern or fear.

Not that James could tell if a crystal squid was afraid.

He stood his ground and continued to fire until his weapon ran dry. Shay's gun roared to life again, downing the few monsters closing on them in the narrow hallway. A burst perforated a squid on the ceiling and its body pinned another, allowing for an easy follow-up shot.

Two charging squids, both rushing along the walls, met their end as James put two bullets into one and Shay blasted the other.

A third enemy leapt from the wall and stabbed at James with a barbed tentacle, a cerulean glow surrounding it. It ripped through his coat and shirt, but the attack only scratched him. He shoved his gun into the body and fired three times. The squid collapsed with a soft thud.

James grunted. "Yeah, I'm adapted to these fuckers."

Shay swept her gaze back and forth looking for more movement, her breath ragged. "Shit. There were a lot more than we saw moving in the room."

"They might have been hiding under the bodies." James reloaded with a frown. "And who knows how many are in the tunnels connected to those holes?"

The squid bodies all pulsed with a bright blue light. James squinted and backed up. The monsters started twitching and thrashing.

"What the fuck?"

"Damn it," Shay muttered. "We can't run. They'd just keep up."

Two of the squids near the back crawled out of the pile.

"Not running from fucking squids, even if they are magical." James grunted and removed a grenade from his belt. "Eat this," he shouted and hurled the grenade toward the pile.

Shay and James rushed backward. The grenade exploded, splattering blue blood all over the walls and mangling several of the squids, their tentacles and chunks all over.

That didn't help. The detached tentacles twitched and inched back toward the bodies.

Whispy's excitement rose again.

Engage enemy at close range for maximum adaptation. Kill enemy.

James grunted and holstered his gun. It wasn't a half-bad idea. The problem with bullets was that they penetrated too well.

He held out his hand. "Give me your sword. If I chop

these fuckers up enough, I bet they'll stop regenerating, and maybe it'll help to use a magic sword."

"You sure?"

"Yeah." James shrugged. "Should really invest in a magic knife of my own at some point."

Shay laughed. "You kind of have one built into Whispy."

Insufficient power for advanced transformation, the amulet announced.

"Too fucking temperamental," James replied. "I can't be pissed all the time."

"Time for things to get expensive." Shay ejected her magazine and slapped in some anti-magic rounds. She tossed her rifle into her left hand and pulled out her sword. "Catch."

James snatched the sword out of the air.

Several squids crawled out of the pile, and surged forward, their tentacles propelling them toward Shay and James rapidly.

Shay fired a single round into the closest squid, which fell to the ground and rolled. She kept shooting while James charged forward with a roar, slicing a squid in half.

Another crawled toward him and launched an attack with three of its tentacles. The latest attacks barely stung.

James cut the tentacles off the squid and stabbed the monster through the body, then pulled the sword out and cut another nearby enemy in half. Shay's bullets ripped into monsters at his side and above him. The blade glinted in their helmet and wrist lights as he sliced and diced the swarming monsters, painting the hallway blue.

The monsters took the obvious bait and focused their attacks on the bounty hunter. Shay continued to pick them off as James stabbed, slashed, and thrust in his attempt to make crystal calamari.

His loud grunts mingled with the crack of Shay's rifle as their attacks depleted the swarm. After a final mighty thrust into a squid, he backed up with a frown, looking for new targets. Several long moments passed, his heart pounding as he waited for a new attack.

Shay had ceased fire. The only things remaining on the ground were piles of chopped-up crystal squids and their tentacles.

She blew out a breath. "That was a shitload of anti-magic bullets. Glad I'm getting paid so much for this job."

James kicked a few bodies and frowned as he waited to see if they healed. "What the fuck are these things?"

"I suspect some sort of magical guardians." Shay shook her head. "Besides the crystal connection, there is nothing like these creatures in local lore. Not sure if you were immune to their attacks because of the traps earlier or just because they rely on more basic forces that you're already mostly immune to." She stood. "At least now we know that if we run into any more, you can chop them up. I'd like to save the rest of my anti-magic bullets. Don't want to burn off *all* the profit on the job."

James wiped the sword off on his pants before handing it back over to Shay.

Shay sheathed the blade. "Those mercs should be glad they didn't come in. If they had that much trouble handling *us*, those squids would have ripped them to shreds." She laughed. "You know, when Erin came to me, I was half-worried I'd end up having to take on some giant despair bug or something, but this job's turning out to not be so bad." She gestured to the golden glow surrounding her. "Haven't even really stressed this ring yet. It might actually last a couple of jobs."

"Let's get going," James replied. "Still have a lot of hallways and rooms to check."

CHAPTER FIFTEEN

A couple of hours later, James found himself wishing for another swarm of crystal squid instead of the endless abandoned rooms. Shay found the few pieces of ancient pottery and reliefs on the walls interesting, but he found himself agreeing with Whispy's general advice. He needed to find something and kick its ass. It wasn't like he was going to find a barbeque truck in the middle of lost ruins.

Their thorough explorations finally brought them to a tall, thick bronze doorway with a brownish-green patina. Worn and barely legible curved writing James didn't recognize covered a wide plaque atop the gateway.

Shay whistled. "Think we finally found what we were looking for. This may be worth wandering around a dark maze for hours and fighting off a horde of magical crystal squid." She looked around, tapping the side of her goggles a few times. "Nothing unusual that I can see. Don't think it's trapped."

James pointed to the writing. "What's that say? That 'Abandon all hope' kind of shit?"

Shay tilted her head. "It's Sanskrit." She pulled out her phone and tapped for a few moments. "Give me a sec to interface with my goggles." She muttered something under her breath and smacked the side of her goggles. "My app's having trouble, but the gist seems to be that a divine messenger entrusted a local noble with a 'holy weapon' to be kept in this fortress until the messenger returned. The messenger didn't return within the lifetime of the nobleman or his son, and by the time of the grandson, it looks like they'd decided he'd return in between five hundred and a thousand years."

"So does that make *us* the divine messengers?"

She snickered. "Maybe."

James grunted. "And does that mean some Atlantean pretended to be an angel?"

"Something different given the local religious beliefs at the time, but same idea." Shay shrugged and shook her head. "But this doesn't make sense."

"Why?" James nodded toward the doorway. "Oricerans did that kind of shit all the time back in the day."

"No, *that* part makes sense." Shay shrugged. "It's Durand. I just don't get why he'd be interested in this tomb raid. I haven't seen anything that looks remotely non-Oriceran. No alien writing. Nothing."

James grunted. "So North was wrong. Even billionaires can be."

Shay laughed. "Good point. I'm just a little disappointed, is all." She headed toward the doorway.

"Why are you disappointed?" James jogged in front of

her. "And let me open it. It'll make your ring last longer if there turns out to be a trap."

Shay stepped back with a smile. "Look at you, being a gentleman." Her smile disappeared. "You're right. I shouldn't have let that woman push her paranoia into my head, but I've wanted to settle the score with Durand for a while. When I thought he was gonna come after me, I was looking forward to taking him down once and for all. But while some idiot mercs could be scared off by a few traps, I don't think he would. I also don't think he was ever here. He might be on his way, but we have no reason to wait around for his ass."

James grunted and tugged on the door, his muscles straining to move the massive hunk of metal. He gritted his teeth and growled, and the door scraped against the ground as he continued pulling.

A triangular chamber lay inside, a stone pedestal rising from the center. A thick layer of dust, dirt, and white and yellow rocks covered the floor. James leaned forward and grunted.

Not rocks—bone fragments.

Slight interest drifted from the otherwise quiet Whispy.

"Huh," Shay offered. "This shit definitely looks promising. Dead people mean something there is important enough to kill for."

James moved into the chamber, checking for creatures or obvious traps. He looked over his shoulder at Shay and shrugged.

Shay stepped inside, shining her lights around the smooth stone walls. There were holes in each of the corners near the roof but no evidence of squids, not even bodies. After a minute of looking around with her AR goggles, she shook her head. "No traps that I can make out."

"They must have been depending on those squids to fuck people up." James gestured to half a skull. "You think these were tomb raiders?"

"Don't know. Despite the climate outside, this place is dry and cool so the bones could be centuries old. Might be people from the imperial period, or might have been treasure hunters after that time, or even poor suckers who just wandered by." Shay scratched her cheek. "Before the portals opened, the jungle would have been safer, too. Well, at least it would have had fewer magical monsters."

James took a few steps toward the pedestal, crunching with each step. "Would those squids have worked without the portals to Oriceran being open?"

"Who knows?" Shay followed him toward the pedestal. "Seen a lot of crystal shit, but haven't seen any crystal lance, and the writing on the outside this room made me think it'd be here."

They both closed to within a yard of the pedestal. The air shimmered subtly above it.

She narrowed her eyes. "Oh, I see."

James grunted. "You didn't pick up anything with your goggles before?"

Shay frowned and leaned toward the pedestal. "Nope. I hope someday they produce a good way to detect magic with a device for us normal people, but until then we still have to rely on it giving off some sort of physical signature." She scrunched her forehead and stood up straight.

"I'd prefer more squid to kill. At least that's straightforward."

James nodded toward the door. "Maybe you should go back there, in case something blows up."

She laughed. "What about you getting blown up?"

"They got their one good hit with that trap. They don't have shit left to get me." James gestured around the room. "Bones, so people died, but no signs of explosions."

"True, but they might not be there after a few hundred years." Shay shrugged and headed toward the door. "But if you're that confident, I'm willing to bet on you. Always made money when I have before." She pulled a healing potion out of her pocket. "I think I'll get ready just in case." She winked.

James grunted. "I'm more surprised there's no King Squid in here to fight."

"These are guardian monsters, James, not some cult or gang. You're too used to fighting organized people and not mindless monsters." Shay leaned against the wall and crossed her arms. "It's not like I wondered if he had a boss when I fought the bunyip."

They both chuckled.

James turned back toward the pedestal.

Minimum adaptation potential, Whispy sent.

That's the point.

James took a deep breath and reached toward the shimmering air. A warm tingle greeted his touch. He kept reaching forward until he encountered something hard and smooth.

"I think I found the lance," he called to Shay.

"No explosions. Good job." Shay gave him a thumbs-up.

James tugged on the object, but it didn't budge. He reached in with his other hand and pulled. Still no movement. He braced his foot on the bottom of the pedestal and yanked hard, grunting as his muscles strained.

The object came loose, and he stumbled back a few steps. A thin light-blue length of crystal with a barbed point that reminded him of the squid's tentacles was now visible in his hands.

James held it up. "Looks more like a spear than a lance to me."

"You're an expert on ancient Atlantean magic weapons now?" Shay walked toward him and laughed. "Maybe you are. It *does* look more like a spear. I think I'll stick to calling it a lance. Got used to it."

"Wonder if we should try this out and see if I can adapt to it?" James asked.

Yes, Whispy all but screamed in his mind. *Achieve additional adaptation.*

Shay rushed toward him and snatched the weapon out of his hands. "No fucking way."

He grunted and frowned. "What the fuck?"

Shay stepped back and rested the shaft of the weapon on the ground. "If the information Erin has is right, this thing has been charging for a long time. Even if it's the same kind of magic, it's going to be at a way higher power level. It's like saying that because a pistol doesn't bother you, you should take on a tank."

James shrugged. "It used to be a big enough bullet would break a bone, but when I went after Calabrese in Vegas, machine gun fire was bouncing off me."

She scrubbed a hand over her face. "You might be the

world's authority on ass-kicking, but as the only tomb raider with a history background in the room, I'm not gonna let you do something stupid like testing an Atlantean super-weapon on yourself." She gestured around. "And Tyler's not here to stream it and make money for you, anyway."

Additional exposure recommended for maximum adaptation.

Sorry, Whispy, but gonna go with Shay here. She's got a point.

Achieve primary directive, Whispy demanded.

James grunted. *Pissing off my girlfriend when I'm close to proposing to her is a fucking dumb idea. I got my own primary directive.*

Irrelevant for tactical considerations.

Yeah, you'll never get a Whispette that way.

Irrelevant.

James chuckled.

Shay frowned. "James, you okay? Kind of spacing out there."

He shrugged. "Whispy was bitching, so I put him in his place."

"Does he ever do anything *but* bitch?"

"Gets happy when I kill shit," James replied.

Shay laughed. "You two are pretty much alike."

"Huh, you think?" James scratched his cheek. "I wonder how it might affect things if I eat a lot of barbeque with him."

Whispy didn't offer any comment. Maybe he was afraid of his host's reaction if he dared question the tactical relevance of barbeque.

Shay smiled at the lance. "Not gonna say it's the easiest

forty million I've ever made..." She frowned. "Actually, yeah—it *is* the easiest forty million I've ever made."

James looked at her clothes. They weren't nearly as full of holes as he'd expected by the end of the raid, though caked-on flaky dried blue blood covered his coat like some sort of amateur attempt at splatter painting. Easy on him, not so easy on his clothes.

Shay gestured toward the door and headed that way. James fell in behind her.

"You know, that's the problem with being some bleeding-heart fanatical rich woman," Shay explained.

James looked over her. "Huh? What do you mean?"

"Erin's obsessed with this thing because she thinks terrorists or spies are gonna use it to assassinate King Oriceran or someone, from what I can tell. I think she's overthinking what happened when the prince was murdered, and the aftermath. Not every assassination is a Prince Rolim or Archduke Ferdinand situation."

"Maybe. Shit's complicated." James shrugged. "Her money to spend."

"I know." Shay shrugged as they passed through the bronze doorway. "I've collected a lot of artifacts in my time as a tomb raider, seriously powerful shit and actual magical weapons of mass destruction. Keys to magical ships and fortresses, and dangerous artifacts that let you control other people's minds."

"What are you getting at?" James looked over his shoulder, still half-expecting King Squid to burst through the door and chase them.

Whispy murmured a few things about fighting stronger enemies before quieting again.

Shay thrust with the lance. "She isn't a killer or even a badass bounty hunter. She might be obsessed with people, but she's still soft-hearted and thinking in personal terms. If she cares so much about artifacts that might lead to trouble, she should be spending money on collecting a lot more than this lance."

"Who knows how much attention she devotes to all this shit? You said she's paying for archaeology research, but her job is running that charity foundation, not cleaning up the world. Probably just fell into her lap and she decided to take the opportunity."

"I shouldn't complain." Shay grinned over her shoulder at him. "This job means I can take it easy. Been thinking a lot about teaching a regular class next semester. Maybe this is a good excuse to do just that."

"If it makes you happy." James rubbed his chin. "Is teaching fucking epic?"

She laughed. "Nice try, James, but you're gonna have to try harder than that to pass your final exam with me."

———

Between already knowing their way and not having to avoid any traps, the trip back to the entrance went quickly. As the rays of sun pushed in from the outside, James nodded to himself. It wasn't even night yet. An evening return flight to LA wasn't out of the question, and fatigue would help him sleep better on the flight back.

Shay snickered, breaking their last few minutes of silence.

James glanced her way. "What's so funny?"

"Just thinking about how I run into all these rare creatures that try and kill me." She shrugged. "Some of the shit I've seen and killed are species that no one else has seen for centuries. It's weird when you think about it."

"I hope most of the tougher fuckers I kill are one of a kind. Wouldn't want to have to deal with He Who Hunts every week." James snorted. "Fucking obnoxious."

They turned off their lights as they closed on the entrance. Something moved in the corner of James' eye as he and Shay emerged back onto the surface.

Dozens of men with rifles and anti-magic deflectors around their neck rushed in from either side.

Kill the enemy, Whispy demanded. *Adaptation potential minimal.*

James let out a low growl. If the bastards had deflectors, they might be better equipped than the first group.

A smug-looking bastard slow-clapped as he sauntered forward. He patted the grip of the bright silver pistol in his holster. "Congratulations, Aletheia. I knew you had it in you."

James didn't recognize the man, but he had a slight French accent, which pointed to one strong possibility. He looked at Shay, who had fixed her fiery glare on the new arrival.

"Who's this asshole?" James asked. "Is it who I think it is?"

"Yeah." Shay gritted her teeth. "Francois Durand."

CHAPTER SIXTEEN

Durand sniffed disdainfully. "After I lost the first man, I thought to myself, 'Why risk these brave and expensive men? Aletheia is coming anyway. Even if she dies, she'll disable at least some of the traps, and she's so talented that she might bring back the lance for me."

Shay snorted. "Funny. That was my plan for you. I'd say great minds think alike, but you're a piece of shit and I'm nothing like you."

His smiled disappeared. "You can't play games with me. Don't pretend you knew I was coming. There was nothing connecting the men you killed to me. I've bested you. Admit it."

Shay threw her head back and laughed. "Seriously? I knew you were coming before I ever took this job."

James' gaze drifted among the mercenaries. Their weapons were all standard-issue AKs, but he couldn't tell what type of ammunition they were using. Anti-magic bullets would get through Shay's defenses even if they didn't threaten him.

The real problem was that the bastards were too spread out. A few well-tossed grenades would kill some on either side, but he'd only be able to charge one group, leaving the others to get shots off at Shay.

Durand stared at the tomb raider, his eyes narrowed. "It doesn't matter what you claim. It doesn't take away from my victory." His smile returned. "Because of the unusual nature of this particular encounter, I don't have to kill you, even though you've proven so frustrating in the past." He gestured for her to approach with his hand. "Give me the lance, and you walk away. Fight me, and you die, and I take it anyway."

Shay snorted and didn't reply.

James grunted. "Do you know who the fuck *I* am, asshole?"

"Of course. The great James Brownstone. You *are* rather famous, after all." Durand shrugged. "Although I'm surprised to see you working a tomb raid with Aletheia. Your presence here explains much of her success, I suppose."

Shay rolled her eyes. "Typical man; thinks another man's responsible for a woman's success. James wasn't around the last few times we tangled, asshole, so fuck you."

Durand flicked his wrist dismissively. "I don't care to argue feminism with you. Just hand over the lance, and we leave. Resist, and you die." He nodded to the mercenaries. "Anti-magic deflectors and anti-magic bullets. It'll cut right through that artifact you're using. An angel ring, it looks like." He snorted. "And whatever you use as well, bounty hunter."

Keep telling yourself that, asshole. You're in for a big fucking surprise.

James gritted his teeth, and his fist clenched. He ached to smash Durand's face in.

"Why are you even here?" Shay asked. She dropped the lance to the ground and pointed at it. "For this?" She let her hand linger near a grenade on her belt. "This shit isn't alien, it's Atlantean. The only writing I found was Sanskrit. Yeah, there was some shit about a divine messenger, but everything in there is consistent with Oriceran influence rather than alien technology. This is standard-issue revised history, nothing special."

A few of the mercenaries exchanged confused looks.

"What, Durand didn't key you into the fact that he's an alien hunter on the side?" James asked.

Durand snorted. "It doesn't matter. They've been well-compensated for their aid. Their understanding wasn't necessary." His gaze drifted to Shay. "As for why I'm here, not everything is about the American government and their little schemes. Their contracts and rules can be cumbersome at times, and when such an excellent opportunity all but falls into one's lap, one cannot ignore it, now can one?" He sighed and shook his head. "I'd hoped to spare you, Aletheia, out of a modicum of professional respect, but it's obvious that won't be a possibility. Besides, it'll be useful to me on those government jobs. You're a nuisance and a loose end, and you've interfered with my work far too many times. It was a mistake to offer you a deal."

Shay snorted and rolled her eyes. "Done with the speech, asshole?"

James' heart rate kicked up, and he glared at Durand.

Anger, Whispy sent. *Hate. Yes.*

The bounty hunter took a single menacing step forward, and all the mercenaries swung their guns toward him.

Good. Point them at me, assholes. This shit's gonna be over soon for you. You picked the wrong fucking side.

"Here's how this is gonna go," James growled. "If you want to have any fucking chance of surviving the next few minutes, you're gonna tell your fucking men to drop their weapons, and then you're gonna get on your knees and fucking beg Aletheia for her forgiveness. If not, I'll rip your fucking head off and shove it down your throat, you fucking sonofabitch."

Durand arched an eyebrow and looked at James and Shay, a faint smirk on his face. "I see, Beauty controls the Beast after all. Fascinating and unexpected."

He pulled his pistol out. Something was off. The front barrel was too small. It couldn't even fire .22 bullets at that size.

James furrowed his brow. A magic gun, maybe?

Shay's face tightened. "I'm gonna enjoy killing you, Durand."

Durand smiled at her and turned to James. "You're powerful, Brownstone. Only a fool would deny that, but you're not a god. You're not even Oriceran, so you will die now." He pulled the trigger.

Bright blue-white energy blasted from the barrel and smashed into James.

"James!" Shay shouted.

The blast spread across his chest, burning through his

coat and shirt and exposing the top of his amulet. Despite that, the impressive display only stung him. His skin reddened, but the injury looked like nothing more than a mild sunburn.

Have I been shot by that kind of thing before? Wait, is it the same kind of energy as that grenade in Vegas?

Yes. Minimum adaption potential. Kill enemy.

Oh, I'm gonna fucking kill him, all right.

James grunted. "Was that supposed to hurt?"

Shay burst out laughing.

Durand blinked, shock covering his face before his practiced smirk wiped the expression away. "Your artifact is impressive, Brownstone, for you to take a direct hit from this weapon." He snorted. "There are many problems with this gun, but I'd assumed it could put you down. Never trust the CIA to design a gun. It's all flash and no practicality." He frowned. "Then again, it could use a second test." His hand jerked up to aim the gun at Shay.

James threw himself in front of her as Durand pulled the trigger. Another blast struck James, more a tingle than sting this time. Before he'd hit the ground, he yanked the two grenades off his belt and threw them at both formations of mercs. They shouted and scattered, a few on the edges opening fire.

The bounty hunter landed on the ground as bullets rained down on him. Two more grenades hurled by Shay flew overhead as the first two exploded, their deadly fragments ripping into a handful of the gathered men, their anti-magic deflectors useless against conventional explosives.

James hopped up as Shay's rifle came to life and put

down a couple more men. He let out a low growl and jerked his head back and forth in search of Durand. His pulse thundered in his ears, and the din of automatic weapons fire barely registered when he found his prey backing away, a reddish glow now surrounding him.

Doesn't matter if you have a fucking artifact, Durand. I'm gonna cut you in half.

Durand's eyes narrowed as James' own found them. The other man pulled out a small white pebble and glared. After a few seconds, he hurled it toward James.

James grunted as the pebble struck him. White bolts arched through him and he collapsed to the ground, his flesh sizzling and his clothes smoking. His muscles spasmed a few times.

Adaptation and regeneration in progress, Whispy reported.

Shay shouted something and held her trigger down, raking death across the remaining mercenaries. A few took the rounds in bulletproofs vest and survived, but her high aim found the much softer skulls of several. Her quick adjustment finished off the survivors on one side.

James didn't care that Durand had managed to hurt him, but the bastard had tried to kill Shay. He needed to pay. He needed to die for that alone.

He roared as the surviving mercenaries fired bursts at him, their bullets stinging now only because of his existing wounds.

Kill the enemy, Whispy insisted. *Achieve primary directive.*

James bellowed and pushed himself to his feet, his chest charred around the amulet. It took him a few seconds to comprehend the pain trying to push through the anger in his mind. Even without the anger, Whispy's euphoria made it hard to worry about such petty concerns as extensive burns all over his body.

Sufficient power for advanced transformation, Whispy reported.

Green-silver tendrils shot from the amulet and covered James' chest, arms, and legs. Claws sprang from both hands, and a blade extended from his right arm. The mercenaries kept up their fire, their bullets going from stinging his burned skin to bouncing off his armor without him feeling anything.

Advanced regeneration in progress.

Durand threw another pebble. It struck James' chest again, the white bolts bursting from the point of impact, but not making it past his armor.

Nice try, but it's time for you to die.

James rushed forward and swung his blade to decapitate a nearby mercenary. He raked another with his claws, then ripped his throat out. The closest men backed up and continued to spray him with bullets, fear creeping into their eyes.

Yet another pebble struck James, followed by a blast from Durand's pistol. He growled. A mercenary near him turned and ran, only for one of Shay's bullets to rip through his neck a second later.

James stomped toward Durand. He was the enemy, and the enemy needed to die.

Yes, yes, kill the enemy, Whispy commanded.

Durand yanked a black rod out of his pocket and pulled on both ends, exposing a silver core. "You can't win against this, Brownstone. It's not human. It's not Oriceran. If you're Aletheia's lover, then you know other aliens have come here, aliens with technology well beyond our own. I don't want to waste this, but I will if necessary."

James didn't care what the fucker had to say. The asshole wouldn't be able to talk once he cut his fucking head off. He continued his advance.

"Fine," Durand shouted. "What a waste."

Durand hurled the extended rod toward James. The core shattered and splattered metallic gray particles over his chest.

Durand laughed. "You're going to be ripped apart atom by atom, Brownstone. They're going to turn you into raw materials."

Nanites detected. Moderate adaptation in progress.

James' armor began to sizzle, and a few seconds later a bright green pulse blasted from it. The silver particles blackened and fell to the ground.

Nanites neutralized.

Durand shook his head. "No, no, no. It's not possible!" He rattled off something in French. "I've seen it work. There's no way you could beat such advanced alien technology."

James continued his advance, offering his enemy nothing more than a grunt.

A few bullets zoomed past him and struck the French contractor but bounced off with no noticeable change in the red glow around him.

Durand backed up, looking more surprised than afraid. "What kind of monster are you, Brownstone, that you can survive something like that?" He eyes widened, and he laughed. "Oh, it makes sense now. It makes perfect sense. You were hiding in plain sight the entire time. No wonder Aletheia cared so much about alien artifacts." Even as he continued backing up, he smiled. "We're at an impasse, Brownstone. I can't hurt you, and I doubt you can get past the magical field I'm now using. Trust me, its history is impressive in who it has saved. Still, it's rare that I'm pushed this far and have to rely on such petty tricks, so you should be proud."

James let out a bellow of rage. Heavy breathing made him turn and almost slash out with his blade, only to stop himself at the last moment at the sight of Shay rushing forward, her hands wrapped around the lance.

Kill the enemy, Whispy chanted. *Kill the enemy.* Kill the enemy.

James held himself in place as Shay sprinted toward them. His hate-soaked mind dimly registered that her glowing aura was gone and blood covered her clothes.

He roared and turned around in search of mercenaries to eviscerate, but only dead bodies lay behind him. He returned his attention to Durand. There was still someone he could punish for daring to touch his woman.

But that same woman was screaming like a maenad and rushing toward Durand with an ancient and powerful magic weapon. Shay completed her charge, the lance piercing Durand's heart. A second later a massive crackling blast of energy blasted from the tip of the weapon, blowing the man to pieces before he even had time to look surprised.

Shay blinked and looked at what remained of her nemesis. "Well, shit. That was a bit over the top even for me." She laughed.

Kill the enemy, Whispy continued. *Kill the enemy. Kill the enemy.*

Shay looked at James with a smile. "Looks like we...win." She narrowed her eyes. "Shit, are you with me, James?"

James stared at her, his heart continuing to thunder and bloodlust bouncing around his mind.

Kill the enemy. Kill the enemy. Kill the enemy.

Shay dropped the lance to the ground and shook her head. "Come back to me, James Brownstone. I'm not done with you yet. We both know you still owe me something."

Kill the enemy, Whispy shouted in his mind.

James growled.

Shut the fuck up, or I'll drop you in a volcano. You ever try to get me to kill her again, you'll see who the real enemy is.

Link error acknowledged. Entering reversion and quiescence.

The blade retracted, and the armor flowed back into the amulet. James hissed as the individual tendrils left his body. He grabbed Whispy and pulled it off his chest. Several long, deep breaths followed.

Shay picked the lance up and rested the shaft on the ground. "Erin didn't say anything about me preserving the charge. It probably works out better that way, considering what she wanted to use it for." She looked at Durand. "Stupid asshole should have never fucked with me."

James sighed and scrubbed a hand over his face. "You okay? You look like you got shot."

"I did, but a potion made it better." Shay shrugged. "Damn, this was a good day. We wasted dozens of mercs, Durand's now jungle food, and I'll soon be making a forty-million-dollar delivery. It feels good to be such a badass tomb raider."

James sighed. "Shay, about what just happened…"

Shay threw up a hand. "Nothing happened. I don't give a shit about possibilities, I give a shit about what actually occurs. You came back to me when it counts, and that's all I'll ever care about." She rested the lance on her shoulder. "Now let's get the hell out of here."

CHAPTER SEVENTEEN

Shay waited in the narrow alley. According to the text she'd just received, her contact would arrive at any moment.

A van with tinted windows pulled up behind her, and a tanned man in a suit stepped out of the front passenger side door. He walked toward Shay's rental sedan, frowning. She rolled down the window.

She'd considered bringing James along for the drop-off, but the last thing she needed was some random middleman seeing Aletheia with James Brownstone. Peyton might think she didn't need to keep a low profile, but she remained unconvinced.

Her blond wig, oversized sunglasses, colored contacts, and face putty would be enough to help her defeat basic facial recognition if the man took a picture of her without her noticing.

The man walked up to her window. "Our mutual friend from the south sends her regards."

Shay resisted a snicker. Everyone had their own

preferred ways to verify things. Since Erin was paying forty million dollars, the least the tomb raider could do is indulge her, especially since the client didn't demand DNA.

"But the north is always a better direction," Shay replied.

The man nodded.

She reached into the backseat and grabbed the linen-wrapped lance with one hand, keeping her other hand on her gun in the seat next to her. "Deliver the money and you can have the goods."

"Don't be concerned." The man nodded and held up his hands. "I'm a wizard, and I'm going to pull out a wand."

Shay narrowed her eyes. What kind of idiot announced an ambush?

"What the fuck?" She tightened her grip on her gun, which was hidden by the door.

"I need to verify that you have the correct artifact," he explained, face tight. "I know the signature to check for. Once I confirm it, I'll signal my partner in the van and the money will be sent to your account as previously agreed."

"Fine." Shay narrowed her eyes. "But try anything and you'll get to experience Atlantean magic firsthand, just like I did on the job."

The wizard blinked. "You actually used it?"

"Yeah, mercs led by Francois Durand showed up, just like your employer was worried about." Shay shrugged. "I did us both a favor and got rid of him."

"Oh, yes, Durand." The wizard furrowed his brow. "Wait, you used it on him?"

Shay nodded. "Yep. Blew him apart. Literally. Pretty impressive."

The wizard paled. "Oh."

Shay smirked and nodded at the lance. "Get on with the verification unless you want me to go into more detail about what he looked like after I used it."

The wizard swallowed, then reached into his jacket slowly and removed his wand. He raised it and muttered an incantation. A glowing and pulsating sphere grew in front of him, its shape distorting over several seconds.

He nodded, and the sphere disappeared. After slipping his wand back into his jacket, he nodded to the van.

A few seconds later, Shay's phone beeped. She glanced down at it and spotted the confirmation of the money transfer.

She blew out a breath. "Nothing like that feeling of getting paid."

Shay handed the wrapped lance to the wizard. He held it gingerly, a mix of fear and awe on his face.

She snorted. "It doesn't matter how old it is or who made it. In the end, it's just another fancy weapon. You let yourself be impressed by that kind of thing, then you're always going to lose to it."

The wizard sniffed disdainfully. "I wouldn't expect someone like you to understand, tomb raider. Magic's not just a paycheck to all of us."

Shay smirked. "Doubt you're working for your employer for free, now are you?"

The wizard sneered. He pivoted on his heel and marched toward the van, then threw open the back door and set the lance inside before closing it and climbing back into the front passenger seat.

The vehicle pulled away. A slight hum from above

caught her attention, and she stuck her head out the window. A small drone hovered overhead.

Like to watch, huh, Erin?

Shay smiled as she leaned back in her comfortable first-class seat. James sat beside her, his eyes closed, again depending on his typical plan of sleeping through any plane flight that lasted more than an hour. People were still shuffling onto the plane. Boarding was taking far longer than she would have liked, but the successes of the day blunted her annoyance.

Why do I care if I have to wait around a little longer? I just scored forty million dollars and I got to take out Durand. Looked like James was going to do it there for a second, but it wouldn't have felt right if I hadn't done it with my own hands—or at least my own Atlantean super-lance.

Shay snickered.

Her phone rang, and she dug it out of her pocket. No reason not to chat when it looked like they wouldn't be in the air for another half-hour at the rate the things were going. Planes might have gotten faster, but boarding seemed to have gotten slower.

She frowned as she looked down at the phone. The call was from Peyton, but she'd already texted him about the payment and he'd texted back to verify it on his end. He should have known not to call with any quick jobs on the way back, given that James was with her.

"What's up, Peyton?" Shay answered, keeping her

annoyance out of her voice. She would at least give him a chance to explain himself before going into bitch mode.

"Where are you right now?" Peyton all but shouted.

Shay winced. "Dial it down there, Pizza King. I can hear you just fine. We're at the airport in Phnom Penh, still getting ready for takeoff."

"Shit." Peyton groaned. "Damn it. You didn't happen to put a tracker on the lance by any chance, did you? You didn't say you did, but maybe your old instincts kicked in and you got paranoid and did it. Did that happen?"

"Huh? If it were anyone else, I'd ask if you were high," Shay whispered. She frowned and sat up. "No, I didn't do that. I delivered the goods, and I got paid. Why the hell would I do something like that? There's still a good chance I can get more work off North after how well this job went. No reason to piss her off."

"Because I think we got played by North." Peyton sighed. "I was poking around some more and managed to trace the money flows. I was trying to figure out if Durand had been sent by the government. There were a few things that didn't add up about the job."

Shay looked back and forth as people shuffled past, some looking tired, others excited. None of the other passengers were paying her any attention, but she kept her voice quiet. She never knew who might be in a crowd.

I not only need better defensive artifacts, but I also need a fancy silencer artifact or tech like North and Goldstein had.

"He said he wasn't working for the government on the job," Shay replied. "And he gave me no reason doubt him. I think he just wanted to grab an artifact on the side, especially since this was a newly rediscovered site. I figure he was gonna grab it and sell it to someone. He might have even sold it to the government and billed it as a powerful weapon they could use against special visitors."

"I wanted to be sure, and now that Durand's dead, I can poke into certain systems without as much risk. I'd already set up searches, and just finished everything in the last few minutes." Peyton took a deep breath and slowly let it out. "It took some doing, and I'll admit I got a little lucky, but I found an airplane reservation to Cambodia for yesterday that seems to be him or at least someone who looks exactly like him. That, combined with some of the stuff I've been able to pull off the phone, has let me have a field day with his personal stuff. It'll take me days to process the potential system targets, but it seems like he was smart enough to keep that phone separate from his government jobs. To be honest, for such a ghost, his personal phone wasn't that well defended. Yeah, it would have been hard to find this stuff out without direct access, but I think he was banking too much on no one ever getting direct access to his phone."

Just before leaving the ruins, Shay had grimly checked Durand's remains for anything useful. Convinced the silver pistol was some sort of government weapon that might be trackable, she ignored it, but she'd grabbed Durand's phone and placed a receiver on it so Peyton could try his best to exploit her dead nemesis' information.

She'd left the actual phone on and hidden in an airport bathroom since she didn't want any of Durand's friends using it to find her once she returned to the US. She figured that by the time they *did* locate the phone, Peyton would have gleaned most of the useful information. He might at least be able to find leads on lucrative tomb raids.

Shay rubbed the bridge of her nose. "Okay, so you found his plane ticket. Big deal. I often fly commercial myself. What's so special about that? How does that mean we got played? I feel like I'm missing something important."

James' eyes snapped open, and he grunted. "Played?"

Shay held up a hand. She wasn't going to have a three-way conversation.

Peyton sighed. "Because I was also able to trace his accounts, including some of his crypto wallets. Because I had the phone data, I was able to associate specific accounts with Durand and found out he got a major payment yesterday. The thing is, the people making the payment weren't nearly as careful, and I traced the money to a Scottish shipping company."

"A Scottish shipping company?" Shay frowned. "I'm kind of lost here. Why would a Scottish shipping company pay Durand to go after an Atlantean lance?"

"Exactly. Remember that I told you about Gordon Anderson?"

"The Scottish arms dealer? Yeah, what about him? He's probably decomposing in Malta." Shay snorted. "Did he come back from the dead specifically to fuck with me?"

"No. It turns out that he used to control this shipping company, but shortly after his disappearance, it changed hands. I'm not going to go through the details right now, but my earlier guess seems right. All my evidence points to the company now being controlled by Erin North."

"What the fuck?" Shay shouted. "Seriously?"

"Exactly." Peyton let out another long sigh. "Like I said, we got played."

Several passengers in the first-class seats turned and frowned at her, as did an elderly woman escorting a young child deeper into the plane.

What's the matter? You've never heard a tomb raider ranting after a billionaire manipulated her before?

James frowned and crossed his arms, clearly unhappy that he didn't know what was going on.

She glared at everyone until they averted their gazes. When she spoke again, she lowered her voice to a near-whisper. "Are you telling me that Erin North hired both Durand and me to get the same artifact?"

"That's what it looks like to me," Peyton replied. "And everything I've found so far points that way."

James narrowed his eyes, his frown deepening.

Shay groaned. "But why? It doesn't make any sense. I get that she wanted to make sure it was recovered, but in that case, it makes more sense to send one of us after the other failed. Not only that, she was the one who mentioned Durand to begin with. She acted like she didn't want him near the lance." She gritted her teeth. "Damn it, you're right. We *did* get played, or Durand did. Maybe we both got played."

"What do you mean?" Peyton asked.

Her heart thumping harder, Shay leaned into the seat and stared out the window at the tarmac. "If she knew anything about my history, mentioning Durand was a good way of getting me to take the job. The only thing I'm not sure about now was her final goal. She might have wanted me to assassinate Durand. Her refugee obsession didn't seem fake, and she knew Durand worked for the government. Maybe she blamed him for being involved in some incident that caused trouble and made refugees? If your mysteriously-disappearing arms dealer theory is right, she's more ruthless than she lets on."

The clack of Peyton's keyboard sounded over the line. "How do you know it wasn't her trying to assassinate *you*? That's the theory I was working on after I realized she hired Durand."

"No reason to send me halfway across the world on a tomb raid to do it if she could track me to UCLA." Shay frowned. "And sending me on a tomb raid means she knew I'd be geared up and on alert. It's probably the worst time to try to kill me, versus just showing up in the middle of a lecture and gunning me down or throwing a grenade at me when I'm in the bathroom."

"You think someone would try to kill you in the bathroom?"

Shay snorted but kept her voice quiet. "Why not? Someone tried to kill me in my kitchen."

"That makes sense," Peyton replied. "But doesn't the same thing apply to Durand? The whole being-armed-and-ready thing?"

Shay watched a meal truck drive toward the back of the plane, her paranoia now feeding the theory it contained a secret mercenary team. Once you got burned, it was hard not to worry about fire.

James continued watching her, a stony expression on his face as he listened to her quiet side of the conversation.

Don't worry, James. No matter what that bitch did, we still came out on top.

Shay's eyes widened, and her confidence waned. "Oh, crap. You're right. Sending Durand after me meant she had to have a good reason to suspect I could beat him no matter what. And I *did* have one. A big one."

"What?" Peyton asked.

"I had James with me," Shay explained. She glanced his way.

He shrugged at her, his brow furrowed in confusion.

"I'll tell you in a minute," Shay mouthed before whispering into the phone, "Any non-dumbass who did their homework would understand that his reputation's the real deal, and he'd be more than enough to beat some mercenaries and a tomb raider."

"There's no way she could know you'd have James with you," Peyton observed. "You don't take him on most tomb raids. She met you at school. It's not like he talks about you online."

"Maybe."

Her heart sped up as various pieces of information floated into her mind. One very disturbing possibility tied together the disparate threads of the tomb raid.

Shay nodded. "Durand seemed surprised to see James with me." She sighed. "But there's one person who knows that I'm both Shay Carson and Aletheia and one person who might know I've had run-ins with Durand; someone who has a vested interest in visitors from far away who aren't Oricerans."

Peyton gasped. "Damn it, are you saying Erin North is the same alien who sent the nanites after James?"

"Yeah, I'm saying it's a good possibility, and a lot of things make more sense if she is." Shay's stomach tightened. "Something felt familiar about her when I met her. The image I saw in Alberta was distorted and only vaguely female and the voice wasn't the same, but there's no reason she'd use her real voice. Now that I think of it, I understand what was familiar about her. It wasn't her voice or even her words. Even the accent was different. It was the cadence of her speech. Something unique about it." She slapped a hand against her forehead. "Damn it. How could I be so stupid? She was getting off on sitting right in front of me, smug and secure in the knowledge she was sending me after the lance."

James stared at her, a deep frown on his face.

Peyton sighed. "What was the play, then? Was the whole thing another attempt to kill James after all? Wendigo 2.0?"

Shay glanced at her bounty hunter beau. "No. If anything, I doubt she thought sending some weak-ass mercs and Durand at us would have worked. I think she, more than most people, appreciates how tough he is. I think the plan was to get the lance. Given what I saw it do and the legends about it, it might have been able to take him down." She snickered. "Too bad I fucked her plans up."

"What do you mean?" Peyton replied.

Shay grinned at James. "Our friend was depending on the lance's charge, I'm betting. Given what we saw with the Wendigo and its changing attacks, she knows about James' special friend and she's obsessed, so she figured maybe she'd get lucky and James would die tagging along with me on the tomb raid. But even if he didn't, either Durand or I would grab the lance and she'd have the perfect tool to take down James Brownstone, with the added bonus of his own girlfriend potentially having helped. Or some shit like that."

James grunted. "What the hell is going on?"

Shay smirked at him as she continued talking to Peyton. "But I used it on Durand, so all those hundreds or maybe thousands of years of passive charging and the decades of active charging were used up. I don't know how powerful it is without a charge, but given what James went through in those ruins, I'm sure he can handle it now." She snorted. "Joke's on her. She might have played me, but I still got forty million. She's got a superweapon that's all but out of power, so it won't be useful against James for decades. By then this shit will long be over one way or another."

James blinked, understanding dawning on his face.

The line of passengers walking past them began to thin, and the noisy chaos from the back indicated the plane was mostly full.

"What do we do now?" Peyton asked.

"Nothing." Shay snorted. "Or just concentrate on verification. Maybe we're wrong, but I doubt it. If she tries to come after James with the lance it won't do much, and now we can go after her online because we have an identity to target. Do your best to keep digging. She'll eventually notice, but now, at least this time, we can go on offense. She wouldn't hide if she could win easily in a fight."

Peyton blew out a breath. "You're sure? You're not worried?"

"Kind of, but not really." Shay grinned. "Erin North underestimated all of us, and that slip up is gonna earn her a visit from James and me."

CHAPTER EIGHTEEN

James stared out the side window as Shay turned her Fiat around the corner. After she'd explained the situation on the plane, he'd decided to go back to sleep. Worrying about the alien woman on a flight wouldn't do any good, and the explanation made his extraterrestrial nemesis seem *less* threatening rather than more. If the alien hunting him was relying on Shay scavenging artifacts, he wasn't worried about her coming at him anytime soon.

I wonder if the lance would have worked on me? I regenerated at the amusement park, but what happens if I'm blown to pieces while Whispy's bonded to me? Can I crawl back together like those squids?

He grunted. It wasn't something he was interested in testing, but his continuously improving regeneration couldn't be ignored. No longer needing healing potions seemed a possibility.

"You okay?" Shay asked. "I get you sleeping through the flight, but you've barely said a thing since we left the airport. Don't worry, we'll fuck that bitch up. We know the truth now, but she doesn't know we know, which means we can surprise her. Then you can go all advanced mode on her and kick her ass all the way back to her planet."

"Yeah, I've been thinking about her." James shrugged. "If you hadn't used the lance on Durand, she might have come after me in Cambodia. Shit, I wonder if she would have tried if you hadn't told that wizard you'd used it. At least this shit would have been over."

"Maybe." Shay frowned. "But if Peyton keeps digging, we can go after her anyway. Erin North might be a disguise for her, but she's a disguise that does a lot of public work. That gives us opportunities."

James grunted. "Not gonna go after her with a bunch of people around."

"Sure, but we'll still have chances. We track her down and show her what it's like to be hunted. Then we finish her off, and we can stop worrying about that annoying new shit you've got going on." Shay grinned at him. "It's not fair that I got to take down one of my old enemies, and you have one hanging over your head."

"Big fucking deal." James chuckled. "If it's not her, it'll be someone else. She's just from farther away than Japan."

"True enough." Shay smiled. "And if she comes after you, you have Whispy."

James shook his head. "When I get that pissed, he wants me to kill everything in sight. He's dangerous. Shit, *I'm* dangerous."

Shay snorted. "Only to people who have it coming." She shrugged. "You keep saying Whispy's dangerous. Shit, you've been acting like that thing is the most dangerous thing in the world since we first met. You've had it your entire life and only started using it to its full potential this last year." Shay slowed to a stop at a red light. "And, yeah, it requires you to get angry, but every time you have a chance to hurt someone you give a shit about, you don't. I don't care if he's the alien devil sitting on your shoulder telling you to murder everyone in sight, you're resisting the temptation. That's all that matters in the end." She shrugged. "You go to church. I'd think you would have long ago accepted it's not the temptation that matters, it's if you give in."

"Yeah, good point." James shrugged.

They barreled down the street. One more turn would put them on James' block. After that quick turn, James frowned as he noticed a dark shape on his porch.

At least my house isn't on fire.

"Were you expecting someone?" Shay asked, slowing the car with an annoyed look on her face.

James shook his head. "Haven't gotten any texts or shit like that."

Shay pulled to the curb and stopped about a hundred yards out. "I might not love this car as much as you love your truck, but I don't want it blown up either, especially with me in it." She put the car in Park. "Let's walk to your porch and see what's up, but I'm gonna be pretty impressed if someone had the balls to come at you at your house again."

They emerged from the car and strode toward James' house, their hands resting on their guns under their jackets.

James frowned more deeply with each step. Everyone

in LA was supposed to understand they didn't mess with his home. Even the Demon Generals understood that. He'd heard that property values were going up in the neighborhood, and he'd had to deal with a couple of realtors calling him and asking him if he'd make public statements of defense of other neighborhoods.

If some fucking level five has shown up to challenge me, I'm gonna be seriously pissed.

As James and Shay closed, it became apparent the person on James' porch was leaning back against the wall, unmoving. The house was undamaged, along with the backyard fence.

"Shit," James rumbled. "Hope no one left a body on my doorstep. That would be annoying. So much paperwork."

Shay laughed. "Probably more annoying for the person who died."

James' hand dropped. He doubted an attack was coming.

"If I can't tie the body to a bounty, the cops will crawl up my ass and all over the house looking for evidence, and we just got back from fucking Cambodia."

James looked around to make sure none of his neighbors were out on the street. If a fight started, he'd need to immediately slam his enemy into his home to lower the chance of innocent people getting hurt.

Shit, but Thomas is probably sleeping in there.

James furrowed his brow. He'd need to smash the person into his garage instead. His dog would probably take the hint and use his doggy door to escape to the backyard. No innocent people or dogs hurt then.

Different tactical scenarios passed through the bounty

hunter's head as they moved closer to his porch. The sleeping person didn't move as they came close enough to make out her features. She was an attractive brunette in a rumpled silk vest, shirt, and slacks, a long coat wrapped around her like a blanket. Her head fell forward as she slumbered, and she had a shiny gold orb in her lap.

James' concern vanished, to be replaced by confusion.

"Why the fuck is Kathy sleeping on my porch?" he asked. "Tyler didn't call me. Did he call you? Or Maria?"

Shay shook her head. "Haven't heard anything from them."

They marched up to the porch. James tugged her coat off and looked her over for wounds or blood but spotted nothing. Her chest rose and fell. He glanced up at Shay, and she shrugged.

James cleared his throat loudly.

Kathy's eyes fluttered open, and she lifted her head. "Brownstone?"

He shrugged. "Why do you sound so surprised? It's my fucking house, not some hostel for bartenders."

The woman sighed. "You need a more comfortable porch. By the way, I think your neighbor Mrs. Garth believes I'm your pregnant mistress or something now. Sorry if that causes you trouble."

Shay laughed. "At least she didn't call the cops on you."

James grunted. "Why are you sleeping on my porch?"

Kathy eyed the orb and set it down before standing. She inhaled deeply and stretched. Her shirtsleeves rode back to reveal a series of tattooed glyphs on one of her arms. James frowned.

"This is hard to explain, but I need your help." She

sighed. "And thank you for coming home sooner than I expected. It saved me having to explain myself again to your neighbors or the pizza guy. I need you to follow me. My car's parked up the street. You can just follow me in yours." She pointed to the orb. "I'd leave that there for now. I wouldn't touch it, either."

James shrugged. "Why?"

"Can't tell you."

Shay crossed her arms. "Can't or won't?"

Kathy laughed. Desperation colored the sound. "I don't know, both? Just follow me. Please." She hopped off the porch and walked toward the street.

James and Shay exchanged looks.

"That tattoo's new," he observed. "And weird."

Shay nodded. "Yeah, and I might not be a witch—and neither is Kathy—but I recognize arcane glyphs when I see them. They've got to mean something."

James frowned as Kathy crossed the street, weariness in her step.

"You think this is a trap?" he asked.

"Probably not." Shay shrugged. "It's kind of obvious for that." She pointed to the orb. "I have no idea what this is either, but I'm guessing it's not good."

"Maybe it's part of the trap."

She looked at him as Kathy continued down the street. "Even if it is a trap, I'd rather just spring it and get it over with. *Fuck*, I'm tired. I was looking forward to a little rest after that tomb raid."

"But we might be walking into some magic shit," James rumbled. "And your ring has stopped working."

"I've got you, and I don't give a shit that you're worried.

When push comes to shove, Whispy does what you tell him to." Shay chuckled. "Just because a dog's willful doesn't mean it can't be trained."

James smirked. "Just not sure who's supposed to be the dog. Let's go."

CHAPTER NINETEEN

They followed Kathy in the Fiat. She took a winding path through town, the property values decreasing with each minute. She eventually pulled off the road and parked in front of a darkened alley in a mostly abandoned industrial area. Shay parked right behind her.

James had already bonded Whispy, who thrummed with excitement about possible killings. The bounty hunter stepped out of the Fiat at the same time as Shay, already equipped with their tactical vests and extra magazines. They walked over to the waiting Kathy.

Neither of them knew what to expect, so James took the *tachi* and Shay settled on her gnome knives.

"So what's the big deal?" James asked.

Kathy pointed down the alley. It ran behind tall double doors leading into a small warehouse, the wooden wall cracked and weathered. A huge Kilomea in a purple suit and gold chains stood in front of the door, his thick arms crossed. He looked their way.

Minimum adaptation potential, Whispy reported.

James wasn't so sure about that. A thuggish Oriceran guard meant others might be around, and Oricerans meant magic.

"Do you know where this is?" Kathy asked.

James shrugged. "Some Oriceran brothel?"

Shay snickered. "That would explain Pimp Boy over there."

"I...can't explain. I think." Kathy sighed and shook her head.

"You think?" James frowned.

"Let's just go in." Kathy looked away. "Please."

James shrugged. "Just so you know, if this is a trap I'll probably kill you."

Shay nodded her agreement.

Kill enemy, Whispy ordered.

Need to figure out who the enemy is first.

Kathy gave him a weary laugh. "Sounds fair. Let's just say I'm not all that worried about *you* killing me." She set off down the alley with a shrug.

The trio marched up to the doors, James and Shay a few feet behind Kathy.

The Kilomea glared at them and uncrossed his arms to clench his meaty hands into fists at his sides. "What the fuck are you doing here, Brownstone?" he growled. "You've got a lot of fucking balls to come to the Eyes' place after what you did. If you knew what was good for you, you would run to Mexico and never come back, you dumb piece of shit."

James' heart pounded, and his face twitched.

Now I get it. The Eyes, huh?

Kill enemy, Whispy suggested again.

Yeah, that's a good fucking idea. Time for a lot of killing.

"Did you just say 'the Eyes?'" James asked.

The Kilomea furrowed his brow. "Are you as deaf as you are ugly, Brownstone?" He pointed to the sword. "And what's this shit? This ain't no movie. You think you're a samurai? That some shit you took from those pussy Harriken?"

"Glass houses, pimp boy," Shay offered. "Or maybe you just haven't looked in a mirror and don't understand how ridiculous you look."

The Kilomea growled. "Fuck you." He pointed at Kathy. "And you're dead, bitch. The Eyes already told us if you showed up with anyone to beat your ass and take you to him. But don't think you'll die nice and slow. He'll make you suffer extra-special for bringing Brownstone."

James stepped forward. The huge Oriceran towered over him, and the bounty hunter continued defiantly glaring up at him.

"Take me to the Eyes right now," James ordered, his voice even lower and more grinding than the Kilomea's. "I have some shit to discuss with him, and it doesn't involve you, asshole."

"The Eyes don't want to see your ugly human ass." The Kilomea flexed his fingers. "And if you don't want you and your pretty little bitch to die, you should turn around and walk away right now." He snorted. "The Eyes might think about forgiving you then." He nodded at Kathy. "But she stays. She owes the Eyes."

Shay sighed. "James, if you're not gonna kill him, then let me. He's getting on my nerves, and I can't get over that outfit. It's even worse than your coats."

James cracked his knuckles. "Nah. Kathy's not the only one who owes the Eyes. *I* owe the Eyes and his people for what they did to my truck." He grunted. "I was gonna handle it after some barbeque, but sooner's always better than later."

Kathy backed away, rubbing her wrists.

The Kilomea and the bounty hunter locked eyes, murder in both pairs.

The Oriceran backed up with a grin and stretched out his arms. "You know what? Bring it, Brownstone. Fuck you. I'll give you the first and last punch, then I'm gonna beat you to death in front of both these bitches. Or are you gonna be a pussy and use your sword?"

James grunted. "Don't need a sword to deal with a piece of shit like you."

The bounty hunter shrugged and leapt into the air, bringing his arm back. He slammed his fist into the Kilomea's face, and the massive guard's head snapped back. He stumbled and fell to one knee, blood gushing from his broken nose. The huge Oriceran shook his head a few times to clear it.

James yanked out his .45 and put two rounds into his head. The Kilomea's body fell back and landed with a thud.

"I don't need to waste the sword on garbage like you," James muttered.

Kathy blinked and ran her hands through her hair. "Oh, shit. That's that, then. Not that I didn't think something like this was going to happen, but we're now officially fighting the Eyes."

Shay shrugged and pulled out her 9mm. "I figured we'd

wait to kill people until we at least got through the doors, but whatever works."

"More of the Eyes' guys I kill, the less trouble they'll be later." James marched over to the Kilomea's body and frowned. "I don't know how you're mixed up in all this shit, Kathy, but the Eyes' men tried to kill me and fucked up my truck, so I'm gonna go in there and make him understand why that was a dumbass idea. This shit isn't for you. It's for me."

Kathy swallowed. "No complaints from me, but..." She sighed. "There are a lot of innocent people in there. I know they're junkies, but that doesn't mean they deserve to die."

James snorted. "Don't worry. I'm only gonna kill the people who try to kill me, and the Eyes. That fucker's going down no matter what."

Hope filled Kathy's face.

"You stay here," James ordered. "Shay and I are gonna go get loud." He marched over to the double doors, Shay behind him. "Ready?"

She raised her gun. "Not as much fun as blowing up cocky assholes with ancient Atlantean weapons, but, yeah."

James threw open the doors and coughed as dense, aromatic smoke poured out of the building. A young woman sat in a corner of the sparse hallway, drool running out of her mouth. Bands of light flowed over her. A man sprawled next to her, staring at the ceiling with a blissful expression on his face and the same light on his body.

Hearing about the people seeking the Eyes' unique bliss wasn't the same as seeing them. James wrinkled his nose in disgust. He'd stick to his barbeque addiction.

The darkened hallway extended to the left and the

right. Different people, most humans but many not, sat in chairs or couches lining the hallway, all similar to the woman and the man, all euphoric and unaware.

I should have killed this fucker a long time ago. I bet this shit isn't just their brains getting rearranged.

Kill the enemy, Whispy agreed.

With a shout, a human thug in another tacky suit charged down the hall, shotgun in hand. He glared at James and his gun thundered and spit its pellets at the bounty hunter.

James grunted at the stinging blast and took a step forward, and the pellets fell to the ground. The guard fired again, and James raised his gun and put a single bullet in the man's head. The brave but foolish guard fell to the floor, a pool of blood forming beneath him.

Shay ran her tongue along the inside of her cheek and gestured at all the euphoric customers. "Check them out."

James looked around with a frown. None twitched, moved, or gave any indication of noticing the gunfire and death that had unfolded right in front of them.

"Huh. You figure a gunfight right in front of them might have woken them up."

Shay's face twisted in disgust. "At least it'll be easy to know who to shoot, and we don't have to worry about people running around in a panic."

"Yeah." James chuckled. "The Eyes' bullshit business is gonna make it easier to take him down."

Heavy footfalls sounded from both sides. Shay crouched by the wall, her gun ready. "It'll be quicker if we go both ways and clear things out."

She opened fire as a human and an elf appeared from

the far corner of the hallway. The human dropped without a sound, but the elf managed a scream as he collapsed.

James turned toward the other end of the hall. "If you see the Eyes, he's mine."

"Isn't his thing being hard to see?" Shay laughed and jogged forward.

Minor adaptation potential, Whispy reported.

Sometimes there are things more important than adaption, like avenging my truck.

James stomped down the hall. The double doors at the end flew open and two elves emerged, both glowing. A faint harsh melody played in the air.

He fired at both, but the bullets disappeared in a shower of multi-colored sparks.

"That shit's annoying," he muttered.

The elves looked at each other and smirked.

The sound of gunfire, shouts, and screaming echoed from Shay's direction. Someone was making her quota, and it was time for James to catch up.

He continued his advance on the elves. They both raised their arms and traced circles in the air while they muttered incantations under their breath. A fireball grew in front of one, and an ice spear in front of the other.

James snorted.

Their magic shot forward and struck James. The fire and ice destroyed his latest shirt but accomplished little else than mild pricks of pain.

Near maximum adaptation achieved, Whispy reported. *Kill enemy.*

The elves frowned and took a step back.

"You starting to get it, assholes?" James shouted. "This is why you should have never fucked with me."

The elves frowned and launched another volley and James grunted as the combined blast blinded him for a brief moment. His charred holster and tactical vest dropped to the floor, the heavy magazines inside thudding when they hit.

James tossed his gun down. "Who gives a shit? I lost my favorite not all that long ago, and I didn't bring along any anti-magic bullets." He drew the sword. "Where's the Eyes, assholes?"

His opponents frowned deeper and performed even more intricate hand movements while chanting what sounded like a wordless melody to him. The bounty hunter stalked forward slowly and deliberately.

He had closed to within a couple of yards when two bright rays of energy, one crimson and the other azure, blasted from the elves and twisted around each other into a single ray. It slammed into James and he stumbled back, hissing in pain.

Minor damage received. Additional adaptation and regeneration in progress. Kill enemy.

James looked down at the charred skin on his chest and back up at the elves. When he took another step forward, the confidence in the elves' eyes faded.

"Wondering why I'm not dead yet?" James shook his head. "Or worrying about how soon you're gonna die?"

They raised their arms again and took deep breaths before chanting a new spell.

"I know what you're thinking," James announced, taking another step. "Some bullshit about your shields, but you're not safe with those weak-ass spells. Not from me, assholes." He slashed with the tachi and decapitated one of the elves.

The blood splattered over his partner, who stumbled backward and slammed into the wall, shock plastered on his face. James didn't even give him time to beg for his life before stabbing the elf through the heart with a grunt. The elf blinked a few times before his head lolled forward and blood dripped out of his mouth.

James yanked the blade out of his latest victim and shook his head. "All you had to do was tell me where he was and run the fuck away. You chose the wrong boss, assholes."

Distant gunfire continued to sound, along with men's' screams.

Sounds like Shay's doing okay.

James marched toward the darkened room behind the double doors. A single dim flickering bulb swung on a chain, leaving more shadows than bright spots in the all-but-featureless room.

A suited gnome stepped out of the darkened corner holding a brass smoothbore musket covered with silver and gold filigree. He raised the weapon.

"Leave or die," the gnome demanded.

"I don't give a shit about you," James explained. "Where the fuck is the Eyes?"

"Die, Brownstone," the gnome shouted and pulled the trigger.

A thin white beam shot from the musket and pierced James' left shoulder. Pain blasted and radiated down his arm and chest. He jerked back and growled.

Yessss, Whispy hissed. *New adaptation in progress. Regeneration in progress.*

The gnome grinned, but James roared and charged. The small Oriceran's grin vanished and he squeezed off another shot, this time striking James' chest and scorching it but not penetrating.

The bounty hunter gripped the sword with his good arm and thrust it into the gnome's head, the tip sinking deep inside. The musket fell to the ground, flashed, and turned into a pile of gray dust.

James pulled out the sword and let out another low growl, his irritation growing with the throbbing pain in his shoulder. He'd grant that the gnome had managed to be more impressive than the other men he'd encountered in the place, but he was still just as dead.

Waves of satisfaction flowed from Whispy over exposure to the new type of attack.

"Where are you, Eyes?" James shouted. "I thought you're supposed to be this super-boogieman badass, but you're hiding behind a bunch of pussy guards? I owe you for my fucking truck. Show me what you've got. Try to give *me* fucking nightmares, asshole."

He looked around the room, but there was nothing in it but shadows, bloodstains, and the dead gnome. Hurried footsteps sounded behind him and he turned around, ready to stab a few more assholes.

A slight grunt of disappointment escaped his lips when he spotted Shay running up the corridor rather than more guards.

James slipped the blade into its scabbard and pulled a healing potion out of his pocket. He downed the contents.

Amulet regeneration might be in progress, but it was too damned slow for his current wound. He still needed to kill the Eyes, wherever the bastard was hiding. By the time Shay got to the room, his wounds were gone.

Shay shrugged. "Not a huge number of guys the other way. Nothing left but junkies and none of them noticed shit. I found a door to the main warehouse floor but didn't see anyone in there. Looked like old tools, mostly." She shrugged. "Think our boy was banking too much on magic to protect his ass."

"He isn't here." James gritted his teeth. "Shit. Is he not here during the day? Did the fucker run? Portal out already?"

"Maybe. Those Council assholes were tough, but they understood when to run and when to stand and fight." Shay furrowed her brow. "I didn't actually go into the warehouse. Maybe there are more rooms behind it, but this place didn't look that big from the outside."

James scrubbed a hand over his face. "Fuck. Maybe I can get Zoe or Victoria to do some sort of tracking spell."

"Don't think you need to go that far just yet." Shay looked around, scratching her cheek. "This room is dark, and there's nothing in it but the gnome. There has to be a reason." She knelt with a frown.

"Maybe the Eyes can't handle light." James shrugged.

She shook her head. "Doubt that. Makes no sense for him to come to Southern California in that case."

He pointed to the dried bloodstains on the floor. "Or maybe this is where they kill people."

Shay tilted her head and stared at the floor. "Huh. I see."

"What?"

MICHAEL ANDERLE

She gestured to the floor. "It's subtle, but can you see it?"

James leaned over to peer at the location. "Just looks like a dusty floor with some blood on it to me. What about it?"

Shay trailed her finger over the floor, following a square pattern. "The dust isn't as settled here. Even without my AR goggles, all those tombs raids make me see simple rooms differently than a bounty hunter. Thousands of years ago or nowadays, people like the classics."

She tapped the floor, which sounded hollow.

A triumphant smile spread across her face. "And there we go."

James frowned. "Fucker's hiding in the basement?"

"That would be my guess, or it's an escape tunnel, but the fact that it's here means the asshole can't just portal out." Shay stood and shrugged. "I don't know an easy way to get in there, though. Can you go into advanced mode and cut the floor open?"

Insufficient power for advanced transformation.

James shrugged. "Not pissed enough."

Shay laughed. "That's a funny thing to hear coming from a guy who just killed a bunch of people over his truck."

"There's being annoyed, and there's being pissed." James kicked at the tile. "And there are only some things important enough to get pissed about." He gave her a knowing look.

Shay blinked a few times and nodded.

"Hiding's not gonna help that fucker, though," James

muttered. He glanced out the door into the hall. "You said there were tools in the warehouse?"

"Saw a few, all old, mostly rusty. Why?"

James glared down at the floor. "Let's see if they have a sledgehammer."

CHAPTER TWENTY

They returned a few minutes later, James hauling a sledgehammer with a smile on his face. Shay was now in control of the *tachi*.

"Keep in mind that if it's a tunnel, he might have already escaped," Shay suggested. "Don't want you to be disappointed. Just because he's a creepy asshole doesn't mean he's a total dumbass. We both killed a lot of guys, and he's obviously worried about you and was plotting something. I don't know what's up with Kathy exactly, but I'm guessing he forced her to bring that artifact to your house, wherever the hell it is."

"But why would she make it obvious what was going on? It's not like she tried some shit and we caught her. She was sitting there waiting to be caught."

Shay shrugged. "Who knows? From what I've heard about the Eyes, plus what I've seen, he might have partial mind-control magic, but it's obviously not perfect. Maybe she was just too strong-willed for him." She snickered. "Or maybe she's more afraid of you than the Eyes."

"Seems like he fucked up this time." James snorted.

"Everyone and everything makes mistakes. Just so happens his is gonna be more serious." Shay tapped the hollow spot in the floor with the sword. "Just hope he didn't run."

"That fucker is still going down, no matter where he's hiding." James hoisted the sledgehammer in both hands. "I'll find him eventually. No way a cocky fucker like that is gonna run from the rep he built up in LA."

"What if he moves to another country?"

James furrowed his brow. "I don't know. Let's just hope he keeps this shit simple for both of us."

He brought down the hammer. It crashed into the floor, cracking the tile and sending several pieces sideways. Dim red light escaped from the ragged new hole.

A few more swings reduced the hidden door to a pile of rubble in a glowing tunnel. A narrow metal ladder extended down.

"All these halls and tunnels," James commented. "It's like this fucker's part rat."

Shay snickered. "I'm beginning to think the Eyes is not the creepy demonic badass he's convinced everyone he is." She shook her head.

"Don't really give a shit." James tossed the sledge-hammer behind him, jumped into the tunnel, and landed with a thud. "Asshole dies either way."

"Catch." Shay dropped the sword. "Whatever the fuck he is, he's still magic."

James caught it by the hilt and Shay hurried down the ladder. At the bottom, she pulled out her gnome-crafted knives.

Shay raised her blades. "Good thing I didn't stop at Warehouse Three on the way back from the job. Not like I carry the sword everywhere with me. Too bad I didn't have any anti-magic magazines for my 9mm with me, though."

"Don't worry," James growled, "I'm gonna cut his head off anyway. I was pissed about my truck before, but now I'm pissed about this bullshit hiding. I didn't think I'd have to drag him out of a hole."

Shay chuckled. "You run through enough dangerous magical criminals, a few of them are bound to be smart enough to know when they're outclassed. Well, smart after the fact. It was kind of dumbass to run your truck off the road to begin with. Even if that wasn't his idea, he did follow up by sending Kathy at you with that orb."

James looked over his shoulder. The tunnel only extended a couple of yards in that direction, dead-ending into a metal wall. He couldn't make out the other end because of the dim red light.

"Does it matter?" he asked.

"I don't care either way, but what are you gonna do if he apologizes?" Shay's eyebrows lifted.

"Fuckers like him never apologize."

James set out down the hallway, his hand tight around the hilt of the *tachi*.

Shay trailed behind him, snickering. "Our last few dates have ended up in dark tunnels."

"This is a date?"

"A couple gets together and does a fun activity together they both enjoy? That sounds like a date to me." Shay shrugged. "Just need food."

James chuckled. "We'll grab barbeque and pizza on the way home. I'm hungry too."

A bright white bolt of energy shot from the other end of the hallway and struck James. The energy spread across his chest, producing a prickly pain but no obvious wounds.

Near maximum adaptation already achieved, Whispy reported. *Kill enemy and find stronger enemy for maximum adaptation.*

Shay crouched, her face tight. "Well, he stuck around."

"Good. Almost proud of him for having balls." James grunted and shook his head. "Whatever the fuck he's using, it's something I've run into before. Most of the magic they threw at me in here I've run into before."

Shay frowned. "Huh. That cuts down on the chance that he's some weirdo freak like He Who Hunts. "

"Why don't you come out, asshole?" James shouted. "Instead of making me dig you out of there?"

Another white bolt zoomed through the tunnel and struck James. He stumbled back, a slight burning sensation at the point of impact.

Near maximum adaptation already achieved.

"I've been hearing about you for a while, Eyes," James yelled down the tunnel, "but I left your ass alone because I didn't figure it was my business. You didn't fuck with me either, which makes you smarter than most of the dumbshits in LA. But you pushed too hard when the cops asked me for a favor, asshole. You should have just taken your shit and run back to Oriceran. I wouldn't have chased you. Not worth the damned trouble. You shouldn't have disrespected me, and you shouldn't have disrespected my F-350. That truck is a fucking classic, and it's hard to find parts, you dumb sonofabitch." He emphasized his rant with a growl.

Shay snickered. "Always good to have priorities in life."

James shrugged. "You telling me you wouldn't have killed a fucker if they shot up your car?"

"I'd care more about them trying to kill me, but I do see your point."

He walked forward. "This shit's gonna be over very soon."

Bright light flooded the tunnel and James squinted. His eyes took a few seconds to adjust. The tunnel dead-ended again about five yards ahead at another metal wall.

Father Thomas appeared in front of the wall. A fit middle-aged short-haired woman in a suit stood next to him.

"What the fuck?" James muttered.

Shay frowned and brought up one of her knives. "Just to be clear, you also see a priest standing next to a woman?"

"Yeah." James wrapped his other hand around the hilt of the sword. "It's Father Thomas, but I don't know who the woman is. Never seen her before in my life."

"Her name is Natalie. *Was* Natalie." Shay sighed.

James glanced her way. "Isn't that the woman you killed the night you faked your death?"

"Yeah. So, what, we're fighting ghosts now? Ghosts are annoying."

"No." James shook his head. "If the Eyes had that kind of magic, it would have come out before. They aren't ghosts. They're nothing."

Shay snorted. "They're obviously *something*."

James locked his attention on Father Thomas and waited for the priest to taunt him or question him about how he'd lived his life.

But nothing happened. The priest didn't move or say anything.

"It's a trick," James growled. "He's trying to get into our heads, like a despair bug."

Shay frowned. "Oh. That's fucking annoying."

Father Thomas and Natalie shimmered out of existence. Durand appeared alongside a beautiful long-haired platinum blonde in blue and Grandfather, the former head of the Harriken.

"Snegurka," Shay explained. "What's this supposed to be, the greatest hits of people we've killed? I don't know about you, but I don't feel broken up about killing Snegurka or that Harriken fucker."

James stepped forward and swung the sword at the apparitions. They disappeared in shadowy mist.

"Come out and fucking fight already, asshole," he shouted. "You think a couple of illusions are gonna make me run?"

Two new people appeared, but James didn't recognize either of them or their species. They looked humanoid and had crimson skin, jet-black hair, and yellow eyes.

Pain shot through James' head. It was as if someone were screaming directly into his mind.

He hissed and collapsed to his knees, *tachi* clattering to the ground.

Shay rushed to his side. "What the hell is happening? Mind attack?"

"My fucking head," James growled. A few seconds

passed before he understood what he was experiencing. "No, not the Eyes. Whispy is fucking screaming in my head."

Shay said something, but he couldn't make it out. The mental noise clouded his awareness.

The symbiont flooded his mind. James' vision wavered, and he tried to fight off the darkness at the edges of his vision.

SEVERE LINK ERROR. CONFLICTING DIRECTIVES. KILL ENEMY. KILL ENEMY. KILL ENEMY.

Another blast of agony shot through James' head, and he howled in pain.

James forced himself to his feet and stared straight ahead. He concentrated on steadying his breathing, then picked up the sword and swung it through the unknown images. They vanished.

Get a fucking hold on yourself, Whispy.

The mental screaming stopped.

Memory restoration in progress for link repair and neurological rebalancing, Whispy announced.

James blinked several times as new memories blasted into his consciousness.

CHAPTER TWENTY-ONE

The young boy crept to his parents' room, leaning toward the half-open door and listening. They had often looked sad in the last few days, especially when they hid in the room and talked.

"I've already seen the orders," his father whispered. "There's no doubt about it. He's compatible with a symbiont. The test levels are high. Very high. They aren't even going to wait. They are going to bond him tomorrow and make him a Forerunner. There's nothing we can do."

The boy's mother laughed bitterly. "An honor—that's what they would tell us. To sacrifice our one and only child. The glories of our lines combined to turn him into a tool. It's disgusting."

His father hissed. "Quiet. What are you saying?"

A loud slap came from inside the room, and his father grunted.

"You're pathetic," his mother yelled. "What am I saying? It's our only child."

"We'll be allowed another after the bonding."

His mother snorted. "Listen to yourself. You've told me these last few years about all your hopes for him, and now you say, 'We'll be allowed another' as if he were nothing. I thought I married a man of strength, not a sniveling coward. And you call yourself a Vax."

"We have no choice!" his father thundered back. "It is the way of things. The strong will survive and the weak will perish. Who are we to stand against the teachings of the Temple?"

"The Vax are strong." She scoffed. "That's what they tell us."

"It's true. The bonded can lay entire worlds to waste. Without the bonded, we'd be at the mercy of our enemies like we were in the past. He can protect us. He can protect all of us."

The boy peeked through the crack in the door. His mother wore an angry scowl and his father paced, his yellow eyes downcast.

"We're nothing but pathetic parasites upon the galaxy," his mother hissed. "The Culling Path is self-delusion—destruction masquerading as protection. Cowardice passed down generations and called strength."

His father stopped pacing and stared at her. "You've been reading forbidden works, haven't you? This is heresy. You'll get us executed."

She sneered at him. "We murder others to protect ourselves, and for what? So our children won't be taken and killed? But our own people take them from us and send them off to fight and die."

His father sighed. "Conflict comes from impurity. Purity breeds strength. And—"

"And strength will protect the Vax," finished his mother. "The

Temple's words are like ashes in my mouth, and I spit them out."
She jabbed a finger in the air toward his father. "Was this what
you wanted? For our son to be bonded?"

"It's an honor," his father declared by rote, but his voice
trembled.

"An honor? They'll take our son and bond him to a soulless
thing that will dominate his mind and body. They even admit it's
soulless." His mother shook her head. "Everything he is will die,
and the symbiont will rule him. If this is strength, I think I prefer
weakness." She put a hand on her husband's shoulder. "It's easy
for us to look at those creatures and think they are the best of us,
but they're a mockery. They are impure. What purity can come
from a thing that constantly changes you and controls your
thoughts? The truly strong would sacrifice themselves rather than
foist that duty on children. It doesn't matter how many races the
bonded slaughter; if this is the way of things, the Vax are
spiraling into weakness. We can't save our people, but we can
save our son."

His father's breath caught. "What are you saying?"

"There are people who will help. We can give our son a
chance to be something more. To be free. To be more than a tool."

"People?" He shook his head. "You mean heretics and
traitors?"

"My highest loyalty is to my family," the boy's mother
declared. "If that means it costs my life, so be it. That is a mother's strength."

"What can we even do?" His father closed his eyes and sighed.
"He's to be bonded tomorrow. Where could we go? They'd
find us."

His mother gave a soft smile. "There's a way, but we have to be willing to pay the price." She held up a small yellow crystal. "They tell us the symbiont is the expression of the will of the divine, but it's nothing but a living machine in the end, isn't it? This can give him the freedom to control the symbiont and weaken its ability to control his mind."

His father shrugged. "To what end? He'll be judged impure, and they'll cull him anyway. He'll still be taken from us."

"Those heretics and traitors you dismiss are willing to help us. We can send him somewhere the Temple will never find him, and if he controls the symbiont, it'll never send the Call and summon the Vanguard. He'll be free, and even if they find him, he'll control the symbiont and be able to defend himself. He'll be truly strong, so the Temple's own dogma would say he's superior." She took her husband's face in her hands. "I can't do with this without you. Will you help save our son?"

The memory blurred into another.

A swirling portal brightened the room. The boy stared at it, confused. He still didn't understand everything his parents had talked about the night before, and when they'd found him eaves-dropping, they'd told him to tell no one or they would all be in trouble.

But then they'd gone into the city, and the blood and the shooting and the screams started. His father had killed a man, but another had killed him.

The boy swallowed, his face's death stare etched in his mind. Why was this happening? What did it all mean?

His mother slipped the heavy amulet around the boy's neck and whispered into his ear, "I'm sorry I can't come with you but don't worry, I will always be watching over you. Be strong, for you are Vax. This will hurt much more than the tests they've done on you before." She slipped the amulet underneath his shirt and the cold metal pressed against his chest.

The boy screamed as tendrils shot from the amulet and spread through his skin and muscles. The amulet sank into his chest, a fiery agony accompanying its fusion with his flesh.

Tears streamed down his mother's face. "Find true strength, my son. Be strong, but most of all, choose your own path."

A cold, harsh whisper spoke in the back of his brain. Pain filled his head.

Primary initiation, the amulet shouted in his mind.

His mother shoved him through the portal.

It winked out of existence behind him.

The boy stood in a strange jungle with plants and trees he didn't recognize. Tears clouded his vision, and his head throbbed as if it were going to explode at any moment.

He kept asking himself the same question: why?

Particles of light danced through the air around him, and the amulet whispered something new to him.

Link error. Adapt. Kill. Adapt. Kill. Link error.

The boy stumbled forward.

"Father! Mother!" he cried.

The particles of light rushed together to form the rough outline of a winged person.

"You shouldn't be here," called a grating voice all around him. Somehow he understood what it was saying even though it wasn't his language. "That portal wasn't from Oriceran. Don't try to deny it. It tastes wrong. This is the problem with you Earth types. It's why your planet is so wracked with discord. There are rules because we want to keep the peace. Who are you that you'd violate the rules and bring your Earth chaos here? Are the Silver

Griffins even doing their jobs? I don't know your peoples well. I believe you are...a Texan?"

Earth? What was Earth? Was that a different city? What was a Texan?

No. That wasn't right. Not a city.

The boy took a deep breath. He didn't know much, but he knew what portals meant. Portals meant not just different cities, but different worlds. Was Earth a planet? Oriceran?

"Where am I?" the boy called in his own language of clicks and hisses.

"Oriceran, obviously, but don't worry. You're leaving right now."

A pinpoint of light appeared in front of him and expanded to an opaque blue circle.

An invisible force seized the boy and tossed him through the portal. The pain in his head worsened, and he passed out.

The boy awoke in a dirt field, a strange city of gray rectangular buildings off in the distance. It was like nothing he'd ever seen. At least his headache was gone.

A strange pale-skinned man with brown eyes stood over him. Was he another non-Vax like the strange man made of light? The Temple said all such creatures were impure.

But were all impure so ragged-looking and dirty?

The boy sat up, sobbing. The pale-skinned man reached over and wiped his tears away and said something in a language the boy didn't understand.

"Where am I?" the boy asked.

The man frowned and shook his head. He said something

loudly and slowly, but the boy couldn't understand the words. He had so many questions. Why had the winged man of light been able to talk to him but this pale man unable to?

Link error, *the amulet whispered.* Analyzing sample. Primary adaptation in progress.

Fire poured through the boy's veins, and he fell to the ground screaming and thrashing. Pale spots spread on his skin, replacing his natural crimson color.

The impure man's eyes widened. He turned and sprinted off, shouting in his bizarre language.

The excruciating pain continued.

The memory faded.

Link reestablished, Whispy announced. *Initiating thought filter.*

James took several deep, ragged breaths. He'd always remembered the jungle and the field, but none of the other things. Certainly not his real parents or some asshole Oriceran throwing him to Earth.

Huh. The Eyes kicked loose some interesting shit.

That meant that decades ago, some poor bum had found an obviously alien being and tried to extend it a moment of kindness even before the truth of Oriceran had come out.

Human kindness. LA managed to have a few surprises left.

Did you keep that shit from me on purpose, Whispy? Shay guessed you'd changed me to be more human, but why?

Local sampling and adaptation necessary for survival in

unknown hostile environment, Whispy responded. *Unexpected neurological disruption during process. Memory pruning necessary to maintain host stability and repair bonding link. Most memories lost irrelevant to tactical effectiveness and primary directive. Other memories disruptive to primary directive.*

James growled.

Fuck your directive. I'm in charge. I don't give a shit what some assholes on another planet wanted you to do or what they wanted me to do. You are my symbiont, and you do what I fucking say.

Link error acknowledged.

Am I a Forerunner now? Is that what advanced transformation means?

No. Achieve primary directive for Forerunner transformation.

James grunted.

And kill the enemy and adapt more to do that? James asked.

Yes.

His parents had obviously hacked the amulet somehow with the crystal in his memory, but it was obvious that the basic nature of the symbiont remained unchanged. Whatever the primary directive was, he suspected it was more in line with needing him to attack other planets.

"James!" Shay shouted. "You okay?"

He shook his head and stood. "How long has it been?"

"I...I don't know. Half a minute?" Shay blinked. "You just stared straight ahead and wouldn't respond to anything."

James grunted. "I'm okay. Just got a little dose of truth. First, we have to do something about our friend the Eyes.

I'm grateful to him for a reason I'll explain later, but that doesn't change the fact that I need to kick his ass."

He waited for more images to appear but none came.

"Fucking magic tricks," James bellowed. "Is that all you got?" He rushed toward the wall and raised his sword, anger over everything blasted into his consciousness. Someone had to pay. Why not the Eyes? He was already mad at the bastard anyway.

Shay blinked. "What are you doing?"

He swung at the wall, and it disappeared in a shadowy mist like the apparitions.

A metal door with a handle stood in front of them and swung open on its own.

James and Shay raised their weapons and took combat stances.

A small barefoot gnome with bright yellow eyes shuffled out of the room wearing only a worn hole-filled tunic. Sores covered his skin, and a few scraggly strands of hair remained on his head. Black blood ran through several of his surface veins. A series of jeweled rings stood out against his overall disheveled appearance.

James stared at the gnome, his mind refusing to accept what he was seeing. Shay shook her head but kept her blades ready.

The gnome took several deep, wheezing breaths and lifted his hand. A black metal dagger appeared. "You're strong in mind and body, Brownstone," he rasped. "Not surprising, but frustrating all the same. I was in your mind before you closed it, and now I see…why you are what you are. Interesting. Secrets beyond secrets, Mr. Vax Forerunner. Who would have thought such a strange creature lived in LA?"

James grunted. "Fuck you."

Shay frowned and looked at the gnome and James.

"But that said, how dare you, Brownstone?" the gnome rasped. "How dare you interfere with my work and defile my home? You had no right!"

"Just to be clear because I don't want to kill the wrong guy, you're the Eyes?" James asked. "Because I want to be very fucking clear. I'm pissed at the Eyes, and I'm gonna fuck him up."

"I have many names. That one has its uses." The gnome waved the dagger. "I am ancient. Your pathetic little country and life are nothing to me. Don't think I fear you because you're not human. I've killed many throughout the centuries."

Shay watched James, concern and confusion on her face.

James shook his head. "Listen, fucker, a minute ago, I would have cut you down like nothing, but I'm gonna give you one little chance because you helped me understand something important. You pay for my truck and turn yourself in, you get to live. Otherwise, you die here and now for all the shit you've pulled, for whatever the fuck you did to Kathy, and for my truck."

The Eyes tilted his head and blinked. "The girl? How could she beat my curse? She couldn't tell anyone."

"She didn't *tell* anyone. She *showed* us."

"Of course. Of course!" The gnome threw his head back and laughed. "So many variables lead to mistakes. It's my own fault. This planet and city have corrupted me. I think too much like you pathetic humans now. So many experiments wasted."

James marched toward him, eyes narrowed. "You give up, asshole? If you're lucky, maybe they'll let you out of the ultramax in a couple of centuries. Or maybe they'll extradite your ass to Trevilsom."

"Enough of your arrogance, Brownstone. You're no longer amusing."

The Eyes threw the dagger at James. It bounced off his head, leaving only a small cut.

Irritation washed across the gnome's face.

"That's your answer, fucker?" James glared at him. "I guess I'll add you to the confession pile for this week."

"You're not human, Brownstone," the gnome rasped. "We both saw the truth in your mind. You're just a cuckoo. A changeling." He let out a wheezing laugh. "A fake human playing at being a man."

"Depends on who you ask, but you can just consider me the best and worst of two worlds." James shook his head. "But most of all, I'm someone who gets to choose my own actions." He thrust the *tachi* through the gnome's chest. "Just like you chose yours. Now face the consequences, fucker."

A euphoric look spread over the gnome's face as he coughed up blood. "I...finally...understand...what... they...felt."

James yanked the sword out and the Eyes fell to the floor, a smile on his face as he stopped breathing.

"Okay, I didn't see that coming." Shay shrugged. "What a weird little gnome. He had all that magic, and he pretended to be something else."

James turned toward Shay. "You could say the same about me."

"Maybe. What the fuck happened there, some sort of psychic attack? And why did you say you were grateful?"

James wiped the blade off on his pants. "I finally understand what the fuck I am, but I don't want to talk about it now. I need some time to let it settle. First, let's get this Kathy shit handled."

CHAPTER TWENTY-TWO

Kathy, Shay, and James sat on Dannec's couch as the elf examined the golden orb, a frown on his face. He'd been all but silent for several minutes, his hand moving and the occasional glyph appearing in the air.

James had no idea what was involved in examining a mysterious magical artifact, so he kept his mouth shut. It gave him more time to think about the memories the Eyes had knocked loose. Now he knew the truth.

Somehow it didn't surprise him. It was like he'd always known. Whispy might have tried to bury the memories, but he couldn't quite bury their imprint on James' soul.

"And your tattoo is gone?" Dannec asked, breaking his silence. "Completely?"

Kathy nodded. "Disappeared when James and Shay were in the club. I'm assuming it was about the time James killed the Eyes, but it wasn't like I paid attention to the exact time. I'm just glad it's gone and all the people inside woke up. That means I'm free, right?"

Dannec nodded. "Yes. The tattoo marks the curse link

for that kind of magic, and it fading after the death of the person responsible makes sense. Still, you're very lucky, Kathy."

"I don't know if being cursed by some insane gnome counts as lucky." She sighed. "It really would have killed me if I had tried to explain, wouldn't it? I wondered if it was just the Eyes playing me, especially after finding out his whole existence was a lie."

"Oh, I'm glad you didn't test it. That was powerful, and true dark magic. It would have killed you, probably in a very painful and messy way." Dannec shrugged. "But you survived, which isn't something many people can say when dealing with those kinds of curses."

James was still processing the memories. Shay hadn't asked him to explain further, only said she'd be willing to listen when he was ready. So many things had slid into place, from why his parents had sent him away to why a random alien wanted him dead.

A Vax Forerunner. A killer. He'd remembered and experienced enough to understand he was supposed to be a super-soldier controlled by his symbiont.

I wonder if those Temple assholes would be pissed if they knew I was using this symbiont to take down bounties and protect people. Is that pure and strong enough for them?

Dannec clucked his tongue and held up the orb. "But this is the real beauty in this situation. Oh, my, my, my. If you'd not killed the Eyes, he would have ended up in Trevilsom for this, if not the World in Between. I'd never thought I'd actually see one of these with my own eyes."

James looked at the elf, ignoring his concerns about his true identity for the moment.

"What the hell is it?" Shay asked. "Some sort of artifact that fucks with your mind?"

"Oh, no. Whatever else our theatrical gnome might have used in terms of magic, this is nothing like that." Dannec narrowed his eyes and stared at the orb. "It's something that most Oricerans would have believed ceased to exist a long time ago. It's a powerful and forbidden type of bomb that feeds off both background magic and souls for its effect. Hard to survive a bomb that shreds your soul. Nasty way to die, and none have been used since the Great War." He shrugged nonchalantly. "Of course, I'm more than willing to take it off your hands and dispose of it for a small fee."

James leaned over and grabbed the orb. "Is this shit on a timer or something?"

Dannec shook his head. "There's residual magic on it, but from what I can tell, it was linked to the Eyes. He was probably going to detonate it remotely using a spell."

"Fine. I've got someone who can handle shit like this." James stood.

"You mean Smite-Williams?" Dannec snorted.

James nodded. "I trust him a hell of a lot more than I trust you."

The elf laughed. "Fair enough. I've earned a nice fee for identifying the curse and this bomb, so I can't complain. It's been a profitable few days for not much effort." The elf shrugged and gave James a merry smile. "If it means something, I'm glad you got rid of the Eyes. Even I'm surprised to find out he was a gnome."

James frowned. "Why? I've run into scummy gnomes before. You're a criminal, and you're a Light Elf."

Dannec shook his head. "Being a criminal is one thing and being a cultist or obsessed with power is another, but that kind of twisted mind? The things he was doing to those people." He smirked. "It typically comes with the desperation of the short-lived. The kind of thing you might expect of say, a human, not a gnome."

"The way I see it, Earth and Oriceran are big enough for all sorts of fucked-up people." James stood and nodded to the door. "I'm gonna go take this to the Professor right away. Don't want some asshole showing up when I'm in the shower and stealing it."

Kathy and Shay stood, both glancing at Dannec.

He waved. "Anytime you want my help, all you have to do is ask. Well, that, and pay."

James chuckled. "At least you don't hide what you are. I can respect that, Dannec."

The elf nodded. "Thanks, Brownstone. Congratulations on cleaning up LA a little more."

"I was mostly pissed about my truck." James shrugged.

Dannec raised an eyebrow. "I see."

James nodded and stepped out of the apartment, followed by Shay and Kathy. Dannec didn't rise from the couch but the door shut behind him.

They were halfway down the stairs when James turned to Kathy. "Never got a chance to say thanks."

Kathy blinked. "Huh? I'm the one who should be thanking you. You saved my life. Shit, given what that freaky gnome was into, you might have saved me from something a lot worse than dying." She shivered. "Nothing worse than an insane ancient being."

Shay grimaced and nodded. "Some guys you kill

because you have to, some guys you kill because it makes the world a better place."

They took a few more steps down before James responded. "You also could have planted the bomb. It would have been easier. It's not like I'm your friend, and it was your life on the line."

Kathy sighed. "I'm not like you two. I like to solve problems with my mind. I'm not going to claim I don't have blood on my hands, because I do, but I also like to tell myself that the person had it coming."

Shay snickered. "I like to tell myself that too. Sometimes it's even true."

James shrugged and grunted. "I don't worry much. People who fuck with me die. Simple as that."

They arrived at the bottom of the stairs and headed toward their cars parked on the street.

"The point is," Kathy continued, "that I might not be your friend, Brownstone, but you're also not a bad guy, and LA's a safer city because you're around. Hell, Vegas is becoming a safer city just because your lackeys are around, and I'm not going to pretend I don't notice that."

Shay winced. "Don't call the other bounty hunters 'lackeys' in front of them. Trey would whine about it for weeks."

Kathy shrugged. "The point is, if I had let the Eyes kill you to save my own ass, it'd make LA worse off, and that piece of shit would have continued being a monster. It was a gamble, but I want to be able to sleep at night."

"I remember when people have my back," James replied. "Even though you did it for your own reasons, you had my back. Not saying I owe you, but you've helped me out a couple of times when you were in danger, and I think that means something."

A thoughtful look passed over Kathy's face. "I'll keep that in mind."

Shay clapped her hands together. "I remember a certain someone saying something about pizza."

James grunted. "And barbeque."

Kathy laughed.

James leaned back on the couch as he patted Thomas, who was curled up beside him. Shay sat on the other side of the dog, skimming through messages on her phone.

"You want to talk about it yet?" Shay asked, still looking at her phone. "I think we should talk about it before we go to bed."

James had given her an overview of the memories on the way back when they'd returned home but hadn't wanted to go into more than that.

"Vax Forerunner," James muttered. "Having a name makes it seem more real. My parents were probably killed right after they sent me off. Weird shit to think about it." He furrowed his brow. "But from what I remembered, that means I'm not unique. Might be tons of badasses with symbionts out there."

Shay nodded. "Are you mad about that?"

"Nah, don't give a shit, but I keep wondering about Whispy's primary directive." James scratched Thomas behind his ears. "If I'm supposed to be running around blowing up places, it probably has something to do with that. They said the Forerunner makes some sort of call to summon the Vanguard."

"Then why worry? You won't do that." Shay shrugged. "But yeah, everything makes a lot more sense now that we know the truth." She sighed and shook her head. "Though I was wrong." She frowned at him. "Don't ever tell Peyton I admitted that. I'll never fucking hear the end of it."

James looked her way. "Wrong about what?"

"Our alien bitch, aka Erin North. Peyton found similar signatures in systems associated with her companies he encountered during our Canada adventure." Shay shrugged. "Erin has to be her."

"But you already thought that."

"Yeah," Shay replied, "but that's not what I was wrong about. Let me back up to explain. You see, everything fits now. When I was talking to Peyton about your past, I half-convinced myself that the alien was an evil invasion bitch and that was why she was after you—because she was afraid of *you* fucking up *her* invasion."

"Turns out *I'm* the evil invasion bitch." James chuckled.

Shay shook her head. "To be clear, I don't give a shit if you're from the Planet of All Evil Assholes—I'll stand with you against everyone. And it's not like you're gonna help other aliens invade, so I won't have to make a hard choice."

James nodded. "Thanks, but will that make any difference to her?"

"It might," Shay replied. "If we can corner Erin and explain, maybe we won't have to fight her. Since you know the truth, we can maybe convince her to back off. If she's after you because she thinks you're one of these Vax Forerunners, we can make her understand that you're not, especially since from what you've said, it sounds like they aren't stealthy infiltrators."

Thomas barked once and hopped off the couch. He wandered over to his water bowl to lap up some refreshment.

James shrugged. "So what's your plan? Call her and say, 'Hey, want to meet the alien you want to kill face to face so you can hug it out, bitch?'"

Shay snorted. "If Peyton and Heather can work her systems, we can figure out someplace to talk to her where she won't open fire. Normally, I'd say let's just go find her and chop her into pieces, but she might drop an alien nuke or something like that on us. If we can talk her down, as weird as that sounds for both of us, it might be worth thinking about."

"Talk it out, huh?" James shrugged. "Wouldn't hurt, but she already knows I'm not leading an invasion and she's still coming at me."

"Fuck, I don't know." Shay sighed. "The initial plan's the same. We track her down and go at her when she's alone. Then we gave her a choice: back off, or we send her to join the Eyes." She smirked. "Time for a little war of four worlds."

"Four worlds?" James furrowed his brow.

Shay ticked up her fingers as she spoke. "Earth, Oriceran, Vax, and whatever planet she's from. Four worlds." She shrugged.

Kathy took a sip of a martini at a table in the Black Sun. They were in the middle of morning cleaning and setup, although the waitresses hadn't arrived yet.

Tyler sat across from her. "Given the shit you went through the other night, I'm not going to complain about you pounding back a few, but getting totally smashed before work is not a good idea. Maybe you should take a couple of days off?"

She shrugged. "What's the point? The Eyes is dead. I'm free."

Tyler nodded. "Then why are you so freaked out?"

"Because I was supposed to be avoiding this kind of crap. That's why I want to be at work. I'd rather keep my mind busy." Kathy set her glass down with a sigh. "I left New York to get a new start and not get drawn into weird conspiracies where crazed gnomes are attempting to nuke high-level bounty hunters." She rubbed her temples. "What would you have done? Would have you planted the bomb?"

"Did you suspect it was a bomb?" Tyler stared at her, no judgment in his eyes.

"I knew it wasn't going to give Brownstone a backrub." Kathy picked up her drink and took another sip. "I'm not a good person, Tyler, but I also don't want to be anyone's tool, and certainly not anyone's damned weapon."

"You're looking at this the wrong way." He shook his head. "Not going after Brownstone had nothing to do with being a good person. It was all about being self-serving, and in our business, there's nothing wrong with that."

"What do you mean?"

Tyler grinned and leaned forward. "Come on, you've worked here long enough to see it. If you bet against

Brownstone, you lose. Always. It's like a law of nature, so I've stopped fighting it, which is why I've got a lot more money now. Even if you had planted that bomb and it went off, I guarantee that asshole would have survived, and then he'd stomp over here and tear up my bar looking for you and kicking in my door and shit."

Kathy snorted. "So you're really just worried about yourself in the end?"

"Like I said, in our business, there's nothing wrong with being self-serving." Tyler chuckled. "No reason to beat yourself up, Kathy. This was a win all around. There's an information void now in LA, and I think I can help fill that with the help of Dannec. That twisted fuck is hopefully in gnome hell, and on top of that, you got James Brownstone to basically say he owes you. That's rare shit. It's practically a guarantee you can get some sort of protection deal for the White Sun, so you can move on to Vegas with no baggage and a powerful friend. Not bad, considering all you had to do was not try to kill someone." He shrugged.

Kathy blinked. "Huh. Every once in a while you say something pretty smart."

Tyler made a face. "Now you sound like Maria."

CHAPTER TWENTY-THREE

James smiled as he stepped into the garage. The F-350 looked shiny and new, not a single bullet hole in sight.

"Everything's up and running," the smiling mechanic announced. "Plus, I found a new supplier who deals in classic trucks, so if, you know, bad shit happens, it won't be a problem getting parts."

"I'm gonna try to not get my truck shot up again anytime soon." James looked over the vehicle. "But as long as there's a piece of this baby left, I'm gonna keep it alive. I don't care how much money I need to put into it. It's one of my oldest partners, and I trust that truck with my life."

The mechanic laughed. "Hey, I'm not gonna complain if you want to come in here and throw thousands of dollars at me. It's fun working on older vehicles, especially with an engine like that. At the rate things are going, in ten years I wouldn't be surprised if most trucks on the roads are electrics. Just not the same; you need to have that…I don't know how to say it."

"Roaring engine," James suggested.

The other man snapped his fingers. "Yeah, that. A quiet truck makes me nervous. She's all gassed up and ready to go." He pulled the keys out of his pocket and tossed them to the bounty hunter.

James snatched the keys out of the air, opened the door, and hopped into the driver's seat, the familiar curves relaxing him. Even though they'd had to replace the seat covers and back, somehow the whole thing still felt like it'd been waiting for him and him alone to come and retake his throne.

My moving kingdom. My F-350.

He chuckled and slipped the keys into the ignition. The truck roared to life, and James grunted in appreciation. Nothing like a beast of a truck announcing its presence.

James waved one last time at the mechanic and pulled out of the garage onto the street. The streets of Los Angeles felt easier and nicer, even more polite when he was in his truck. He didn't give a shit if that was his mind playing tricks on him.

What kind of truck would I get if something happened to this one? A newer Ford? Shit, I don't know.

Shay didn't understand. She had an entire warehouse annex filled with different cars. Even if she drove the Fiat most of the time, her vehicle wasn't the same kind of partner to her as James' Ford was to him, and unlike Whispy Doom, the damned truck didn't talk back or hide memories from him.

James patted his chest, the familiar weight of the amulet resting on his skin. Shay had in many ways been more curious about his past than he was. He had better insight into it now, but as far he was concerned, it didn't make any difference.

He'd been on Earth for decades, and the Vax hadn't come looking for him. His people might be zealots raining bonded symbiont fire upon the rest of the galaxy, but they might as well be extinct for all the difference it made to his life. For all Whispy's bitching, the symbiont followed his orders, so it didn't matter what the true nature of its primary directive was.

I'm never giving the call, whatever the hell that is, so he'll be fucking whining for the next fifty years. That shit's gonna get annoying.

James grunted and shook his head. No reason to think about a situation he couldn't control. It did nothing but make his life more complicated. For now, he could soak in the simple pleasures of a nice truck, a loving daughter, and a kickass girlfriend.

For a long time, he hadn't lived; he'd simply existed. Now when he woke up, he had a reason, focus, and people he gave a shit about. Not just a family, but true friends. Before he'd felt satisfaction. Now he felt damned happy.

James chuckled at a sudden thought about the mysterious Vanguard.

Could Whispy adapt to attack another Vax bonded to a symbiont? I bet Tyler would love to run a pay-per-view event with that fight card.

Maybe I'll ask Whispy next time we're bonded. How's that for adapting and becoming stronger?

James' phone rang, and he grabbed it. Unknown number.

Don't fuck with my good mood, whoever you are.

He brought the phone to his ear after he turned at an intersection. "This is Brownstone."

"Say what you need to say, big boy," came a woman's voice.

Even though James hadn't heard it in a long time, much like faces, he never forgot a voice.

He sighed. "Do we really need to do this shit, Addie? You know who the fuck I am."

She laughed. "Do I? You could be some elf running a spell for all I know, and you know how I work, Mr. Brownstone. The Professor told me he gave you the first and second passphrases. You don't use them, I hang up and abort the drop to renegotiate with the Professor."

"That's bullshit, since he made it sound like this was all you this time." James grunted and rolled his eyes. "At least it's not a fucking limerick this time."

"Ten seconds, Mr. Brownstone. Nine, eight, seven…"

"Fine. Fucking Professor." James gritted his teeth and took a deep breath. He'd almost prefer a dirty limerick to the passphrase he was about to say. It was wrong on so many levels. "Chevys are better than Fords."

Addie let out another laugh. "Verified. Secondary passphrase will be needed on delivery, along with DNA confirmation. Understood?"

"Yeah, I understand." James' other hand tightened on the wheel. "If you're making me do all this shit, that means you're in town right? This delivery's gonna be soon?"

"Yep." The courier rattled off an address in Encino. "It's a drive-in. Nice and empty during the day, and I like that for high-risk jobs."

"You don't want people around?"

Addie blew out a breath. "Nope, not for this job. Lots of nasty people who might fuck with me, but I've managed to lose them all so far. Still, can't be too careful. Just unprofessional to get people caught up in your work crap."

James grunted. "Yeah, I know what you mean."

"I'll be there in one hour, and I'll wait exactly fifteen minutes. Then I'll leave, and I'll renegotiate with the Professor."

James frowned and took a right at the next intersection. He needed to turn around immediately. "Not into the customer service, are you, Addie?"

"No, you've got it all wrong, Mr. Brownstone," she replied. "It's totally the opposite. If someone hires me, it's because it's not like they can just ship the package through Andercarr or FedEx. That usually means they need to get something from point A to point B, but there's a good chance someone really dangerous wants it. I know the last time we worked together was kind of a strange thing, but don't misunderstand. I *want* to deliver this stuff to you. I love a good courier job, and while I am a sexy and awesome courier, unlike you, I'm not a walking tank."

"I'll be there on time. Don't worry." James took a deep breath. It wasn't like he could miss out on his opportunity to grab Shay's engagement ring and matching pendant. They were perfect for her.

"I'm not a total bitch, and I get this is LA. If you hit traffic, let me know and I'll pick a new rendezvous point. We don't need to go through the Professor for that. See you soon, big boy."

Addie hung up.

James turned again and was now heading north. He should have plenty of time, provided LA cooperated.

Luck, or maybe Saint Christopher, was with James as the snarling beast called Los Angeles traffic slept. He made decent time, and he spotted the road turning into the drive-in. After his turn, the road split into several lanes leading to separate free-standing ticket booths and a small side parking lot.

James frowned as he looked into the parking lot. He grunted and hit the brakes, the truck screeching to a halt. Addie's black Porsche was parked in the lot, but two blue SUVs had her vehicle pinned. Even at a distance, James could make out Addie's bright green hair as she sprinted toward the ticket booths. A dozen men in dark suits chased her, sunlight glinting off the guns in their hands.

He snorted.

Guess she had a point about why people need to hire her and picking a place without a lot of people.

James didn't know what the Professor had her carrying, but he wasn't about to let random thugs steal Shay's engagement ring.

He threw open his door and jumped out. A brief thought about bonding Whispy passed through his mind.

Nah. I'll use him when I need him. Don't need him for these assholes. They're all humans, and they've got guns, no wands. If I can't take them without Whispy, I'm a pussy.

The loud crack of gunfire sounded. Bullets sparked as they struck the ground near the fleeing courier. Addie glowed for a second, then a half-dozen copies of her appeared and ran in different directions.

Nice one. Is she a witch or was that an artifact?

James threw open the back door and reached into his go case for a few extra magazines. He stuffed them in his pockets, unholstered his gun, and ran toward the ticket booths.

That's a lot of guys for one courier.

The thugs continued firing at the pack of Addison Endos, not noticing James. Several of the identical women disappeared in puffs of smoke as bullets struck them. The continuing fire soon eliminated all but the real Addie.

She reached the first ticket booth and snaked around the side, achieving decent cover.

Now that James was closer, he could see she wore a small backpack over her white jacket along with black tights, a mesh tank top, and sneakers.

It's like she knew she was gonna have to run. More practical clothes than the dress she was in last time we met.

Addie reached into her jacket and pulled out a pistol. She whipped a few quick shots around the corner, but the barrage from her pursuers forced her back. A quick sprint sent her to the next ticket booth.

James fired his .45 at the men as he arrived at a ticket booth. Two of them fell to the ground screaming and the remaining men scattered, half rushing in Addie's direction and the others at him. Their shots flew wild, no one aiming well in their panic.

Pathetic. These aren't pros if one guy dying makes them lose their shit. Maybe just some cocky mobsters who aren't used to dealing with real trouble.

James grinned at the thought and flattened himself against the wall of the ticket booth. Bullets whizzed past, and a few ripped through.

Good thing no one has a big gun.

He ducked around the wall and squeezed off a few rounds at the charging crew. Another of the thugs took two rounds to the chest and fell. The bounty hunter turned and fired at the crew pursuing Addie and nailed a surprised man in the head.

Addie zigzagged and fired wildly as she sprinted toward James' position. He kept up his cover fire and the thugs ducked behind other ticket booths, several shouting. The courier dove and rolled as another few rounds of bullets came her way and ended up a few feet from James with nothing worse than a slight tear in her tights.

The lithe courier sprang to her feet with practiced ease. "Sorry about the lack of warning, Mr. Brownstone. They rolled up on me before I could get a message off." Her cheeks colored. "Kind of embarrassing."

"Shit happens, and fuckers can get the drop on anyone." James grunted. "Any idea who they are?"

Several more bullets perforated their booth.

Addie shrugged. "Assholes? They didn't introduce themselves. The minute they pulled up, I got out of my car and started running. I'm pretty good at knowing when to run and when to stand and snark. Maybe in Bounty Hunter Land you always know who you're dealing with, but as a high-end courier, you'd be surprised how often random strangers try to kill you. I take it in stride these days." She patted the backpack. "The important thing is the cargo."

More bullets pelted the booth.

"It's not so different for me," James responded.

During a lull in enemy shots, he popped from cover to fire. A cocky thug had left his cover and received several rounds in the chest for his arrogance.

The bounty hunter ejected his magazine and reloaded. "Only seven left. I don't know if they're idiots who should have more discipline or brave fuckers for not cutting and running."

Addie fired a few quick shots of her own around the corner and laughed. "Yeah, this is not what I'd call a fun day, and I'm a big believer in smart people understanding that discretion is the better part of valor." She nodded at her backpack. "Don't worry, I've got the items. I'd give them to you, but we still need to do the DNA verification, so I can't just hand them over."

James snorted. "I'm helping you in a gunfight! Doesn't that prove anything?"

"Verification is how I do things, big boy." Addie fired a few more times and her gun ran dry. She yanked a new magazine out of her jacket and slapped it in. "Don't have a huge number of spare mags, but don't worry. If they kill me, you can just take the backpack and run. Might have some trouble with the locks, though."

"I'm just gonna finish this shit so you can give me the crap." James moved toward her. "Switch places with me, and lay down some cover fire. It's time I showed these fuckers who they're dealing with."

Addie circled around James and nodded, lifting her gun with both hands.

A few more bullets ripped through the ticket booth.

There were now enough holes that they could see movement through the back wall.

"Three," James began, "two, one…"

Addie aimed around the corner and sent round after round toward the men clustered at the far booth.

I wish I had a grenade on me. It'd be easy to end this shit then.

James took his opportunity and rushed toward the next closest booth. He didn't fire, instead holstering his pistol and jumping. His hands caught the edge of the angled roof, and with a yank, James pulled himself on top of the booth. While Addie continued firing, James rushed forward and jumped onto the next roof.

The confused men hesitated, some looking up at James and others still engaging Addie, which was a mistake. That cost one of the men his life as the courier shot him in the neck.

The loud thud of James' mass of muscle landing on the top of their ticket booth forced the surviving men to focus on the approaching bounty hunter. He didn't open fire or slow before hurling himself off the top and slamming a fist into one of the men on his way down. The thug crashed into two of his friends, and all three collapsed with groans.

James threw an uppercut into the next closest man. The target flew backward, his head hitting the wall behind him with a loud pop. He sank to the ground, his head at an odd angle and his eyes locked in a death stare.

The bounty hunter barreled into the remaining men and tackled them to the hard asphalt. One of the man's eyes rolled up in the back of his head and blood leaked from the back of his split skull. A few more hard punches sent his friend to the same fate.

The survivors disentangled themselves from James' first victim as he pulled his .45. He squeezed the trigger one time for each man, putting bullets into their heads.

He didn't know these men or why they were after Addie's cargo, and he didn't care. They were fucking with him picking up Shay's engagement ring; that was all he needed to know.

James chuckled. Weddings and marriage were the ultimate in complicated.

He waited, gun out. The men all looked like normal if well-dressed human thugs, the type you might see any random organized crime group send out, but he couldn't ignore the possibility that someone might start regenerating or turn out to be a secret gnome.

Nothing like that happened. They all stayed conveniently dead.

"Huh. Sometimes shit *does* work out." James shrugged. "You okay, Addie?" he shouted.

"I didn't get hit," she called back.

"You see anyone else?"

Addie poked her head around the corner of her booth. "Looks clear. Thanks, Mr. Brownstone." She took a deep breath and jogged toward him. "Things got a little tense there. I prefer outrunning people in my car." She nodded toward the Porsche in the distance. "I was half worried they'd shoot it up."

James grimaced. "I can relate to that." He nudged a body with a foot. "You need to search these guys or anything?"

Addie furrowed her brow. "Why?"

"To grab IDs, figure out who sent them—that kind of shit." James shrugged.

"Don't really care who they are." Addie squatted by a man with a frown. "Assholes like this generally don't care if they've messed up a delivery." She grinned up at him, amusement in her one green eye and one blue eye. "Couriers aren't like bounty hunters, Mr. Brownstone. Even a lot of criminal types might need our services, so they don't tend to hold grudges, even if some of their guys get killed trying to mess with one of us."

"You do jobs for criminals?"

Addie stood and nodded. "I don't choose them, but I do take a lot of blind jobs. The Professor likes to fill me in on details, but not every client does. If someone hands me a box and tells me not to look inside, I don't look inside. That's rule number one of being a high-risk courier. But now that we're done with that...unpleasantness, let's get down to business." She reached into her pocket and pulled out a small metallic square plate. "Your thumb, please, Mr. Brownstone."

James grunted and placed his thumb on the DNA reader. After a faint burn, it beeped.

Addie smiled. "And the secondary passphrase."

He stared at her. "Even though you just did a DNA scan?"

"Yep. One time I was on a job in Bogota and the primary passphrase was verified, DNA matched, every-thing. Then at the last minute, the guy doesn't know the secondary passphrase." Addie shrugged. "Turns out there was a spell on him, and some warlock was ready to snatch the package. So verification, please."

James sighed. "Hyundai is better than Ford." He groaned. "Fucking Professor. I should make him drink nothing but fucking tea for a month for making me say that kind of shit."

Addie stuck the DNA reader back in her pocket and unzipped her backpack. She pulled out a small black case with a built-in DNA reader on it and placed her thumb on it. The box clicked, and she opened it to reveal a small but tasteful jade pendant and a matching ring nestled in velvet.

She smiled. "Your items, Mr. Brownstone."

James plucked out the jewelry and put the pieces into his jacket pocket. Addie closed the box and put it back into her backpack before retrieving another small box and handing it to Brownstone.

"That's for the Professor," she explained. "It's DNA-keyed to him already."

They both snapped their heads around as another blue SUV roared into the parking lot. It braked hard and swerved to the side, then the doors flew open and several more suited men jumped out, guns at the ready.

Addie sighed and zipped up her backpack. "Never ends on some days. You'd think if they sent twelve guys, they would have figured that would be enough."

James handed the box back to her. "Don't worry. I've got this." He marched toward the men as they hopped out of the vehicle. All six pointed their guns at him.

"Woah, Mr. Brownstone," Addie called. "Uh, what the hell are you doing?"

James shrugged and continued walking. "Feeding my adoring fucking public." He stopped about ten yards from

MICHAEL ANDERLE

the men, who watched him warily. "Do you know who the fuck I am?" he shouted.

The men frowned and exchanged looks. They kept their guns trained on him.

One of the men's faces twitched, and his gun wavered. "That's James Brownstone. Fuck."

"Seriously?" one of the other men asked. "No way that's him. The boss didn't say anything about Brownstone being involved. Why would he even care?"

"Because the courier was carrying shit for me." James pointed at the nearest pile of bodies. "You think those fuckers killed themselves?" He gestured to Addie. "Or that she killed them all?"

Several of the men visibly swallowed or paled. Several more cursed under their breath.

James grunted. "Don't know who you are. Don't fucking care. I came here to pick something up and a bunch of those assholes were fucking with the courier making the delivery, which makes me think they were going to steal shit that belongs to me. Now you've got to ask yourself an important question: do you want to be the assholes who try to steal from James Brownstone?"

"Fuck," one of the men shouted. "This isn't worth it." He holstered his gun and climbed back into the car.

The driver glared at him. "Come on, we have our orders from the boss. It's just one guy."

"I'm sure that was what the Harriken said," another man commented and stepped into the SUV.

"And the Council," a third offered before retreating.

Two of the three remaining men shook their heads and holstered their weapons before climbing back into the

SUV. Only the red-faced driver remained, but even he'd lowered his gun.

"Come on, Brownstone," the man shouted, "maybe we can make a deal. I don't know what that bitch is carrying, but we don't need all of it. We didn't come here to steal from you. We've just got a job to do. Nothing personal."

"Stealing from me *is* fucking personal." James flexed his fingers at his sides. "Get the fuck out of here. I don't like killing people who don't have bounties. It's a waste of time, but I make an exception for people who fuck with me and make my day more annoying."

"Fuck it. It's not worth the trouble to fuck with you, Brownstone. My boss will understand." The driver frowned and holstered his weapon. "I'm gonna tell him you killed those guys though."

James shrugged. "Big fucking deal. I did."

The driver shook his head, jumped into the vehicle, and slammed the door. A few seconds later, the SUV peeled out of the parking lot.

"That's some proper respect there," James rumbled.

"Damn!" Addie walked to his side. "You basically just yelled at those guys and made them run. I think I'm more impressed by that than the guys you killed." She held out the box.

James took the box. "The guys I killed were dumbasses. The guys who ran were smart. It's like you said—sometimes you need to know when to run."

"Thanks anyway, Mr. Brownstone. Remember, if you ever need a courier, the Professor knows how to get hold of me. I like your style." Addie waved and jogged toward her Porsche, then stopped and ran toward the bodies.

"Probably going to need keys to move the SUVs." She laughed.

James watched her for a few seconds before reaching into his pocket to pull out the ring and pendant. He held them up, and the afternoon sun produced a bright halo around the jewelry.

I've got an epic engagement ring now, but I still need a fucking epic proposal.

CHAPTER TWENTY-FOUR

J ames sat down across from the Professor and set the box in front of him. "That was some annoying shit."

The Professor took a sip of his drink and smiled. "Yes, Miss Endo informed me that some unpleasant men interrupted her delivery, but I knew it was nothing you couldn't handle, lad. That was why I asked you to be involved."

James shrugged. "Most of the people who showed up are dead. She said I didn't need to worry about them. That still the case? Don't care much, but it's nice to know who's closer to the top of the list of 'assholes who want to kill James Brownstone.'"

The older man shook his head. "You're fine, lad. I doubt any of the men left alive will dare even look at you on tv again." He patted the box. "Unfortunately, the tomb raider who acquired this for me has a loose tongue. I won't be using him again. Alas, not everyone can be as skilled and conscientious as Miz Carson." He gulped some more beer. "You received the ring and the pendant, I take it?"

James fished them out of his pocket and set them on the table.

The Professor smiled and nodded. "Very pretty. Very nice." He lifted the pendant. "To be clear, both produce a visible magical force field when used, but when they are worn simultaneously, it's even stronger. They require an Old Mandarin passphrase to activate and deactivate. I'll send you a recording on your phone, along with phonetic information you can pass along to Miz Carson. If their defenses are exceeded, nothing bad happens to the artifacts; they simply stop working until recharged. The only trick with them is that they require moonlight to recharge. Direct moonlight charges them faster, but they'll charge even under cloud cover, just slower." He set the pendant back down. "I think Miz Carson will appreciate both their aesthetic and utility values. That said, a ring, even a magic one with a matching pendant, requires an adequate proposal. How are you coming with that?"

"Halfway." James shrugged. "Haven't worked it out all the way, but I've got an idea at least."

"Oh?" The Professor raised an eyebrow. "An idea? That's promising. What sort of idea?"

"Something to do with a tomb raid; just need to find the right one with the right atmosphere." James shrugged. "Probably need Heather and Peyton to help me, along with some advice from Alison."

The Professor chuckled. "I'm more than happy to help you as well, lad. Once you have a more concrete idea what you're looking for, let me know and I'll see what I can do. I'm sure we can be of use to one another."

"Thanks, Professor." James stood and nodded at the box. "Hope you enjoy whatever that is."

"Oh, no, James. This I intend to bury somewhere very deep and far away." A pained smile appeared on his face. "As your experience with the Eyes recently reinforced, some artifacts simply shouldn't exist."

"Have fun burying it, then." James nodded slowly and pushed his chair in. "See you later."

"Have a good afternoon, lad."

Shay frowned at her phone as the news video played. She'd decided to check the news before bed and was skimming headlines as James brushed his teeth in the bathroom. She hadn't expected what she was seeing.

The yellow chyron at the bottom cut straight to what she cared about: ERIN NORTH, INTERNATIONAL REFUGEE ADVOCATE, KILLED IN PLANE CRASH.

In the video, dozens of firefighters stood around the smoldering wreck of a small private jet on a runway. A reporter stood behind the line of police keeping curious onlookers at bay. Several ambulances were parked off to the side, but their open backs revealed no patients.

The image shifted to an overhead view from a circling drone. Pieces of the jet were scattered up and down the runway.

"Again, we're having trouble confirming all the details," explained the reporter in voiceover, "but we can confirm at this time that a private jet carrying Erin North, CEO of the Global Empathy Foundation, crashed after an apparent engine failure while landing at Chicago O'Hare. Witnesses have reported that the plane seemed to be out of control and unpowered when it fell from the sky, and we've received initial reports that air traffic controllers lost contact with the plane before the crash.

"While no one on the ground was hurt and no other planes were damaged in the crash, the private jet was completely destroyed. As you can see, there are fragments all over the runway. First responders have already recovered at least two bodies from the plane and authorities are still combing the wreckage for more."

Shay narrowed her eyes.

No fucking way. No fucking way in hell.

She scrubbed a hand over her face.

"Authorities have confirmed that Erin North was killed in the crash," the reporter continued. "At this time, it's presumed the other body is the pilot of the plane, but that hasn't been verified. We have no information at this time about the cause of the crash, but Miss North has received numerous death threats from militant groups angry about her foundation's work. It's not beyond the realm of possibility that this was a targeted assassination brought on by sabotage. Some have already suggested that the unpowered descent might be linked to a directed EMP attack."

The video shifted back to a ground-level view. Suited agents, both men and women, climbed out of black SUVs with US government plates.

The camera shifted to the pale and harried-looking reporter. "I've just been informed that local PDA agents have arrived to perform the initial magical scans. Let me stress that at this time there is no indication that magic was involved in the destruction of this plane, but at the same time, we don't know the cause. FBI and NTSB investigators are reported to be en route but have yet to arrive, to the best of our knowledge."

Shay paused the video and sighed. "Fuck, fuck, *fuck*. Fuck me." She groaned loudly.

James emerged from the bathroom in just his boxer shorts. His shirtless form displayed all his tattoos and abs that were probably illegal in twenty states. "Woah, slow down there, Shay. I haven't even gotten to bed yet. Give me a minute."

She shook her head. "Not that I don't want a little of that, but according to the news, Erin North just died in a plane crash. A rather mysterious and conveniently-timed plane crash."

James frowned and sat down on the bed. "Shit. Seriously?"

"Yeah, seriously." Shay set her phone down on the nightstand. "I don't believe that for a second. Little Miss Nanoform gets taken out in a plane crash? Bullshit."

"Being an alien doesn't mean she can't die in a plane crash. If I didn't have Whispy bonded to me, I couldn't survive one, and I'm not sure I could even with him." James shrugged and nodded toward the amulet, which lay on the nightstand on his side of the bed. "Not gonna try that shit out anytime soon."

Shay sighed. "The thing is, Peyton told me that things have gotten really quiet with North in the last few days. He used the words, 'suspiciously quiet.'"

James frowned. "Now that you mention it, Heather said something about that too. She thought maybe North was lying low for a while because she knew they were poking around."

"Exactly, but what better way to lie low than fake your death?" Shay snorted. "I should know; I'm a fucking expert on that shit." She gritted her teeth. "Damn it. We pushed too hard and lost our window of opportunity. The bitch must have realized we figured it out and decided to disappear."

James eyed the amulet on the nightstand for a few seconds before returning his attention to Shay. "She's pulling an Eyes, then. She's afraid. That means she doesn't think she can take me, not even if she has people she can hire, and the lance isn't charged anymore. Her only choice was to fake her death and run away."

"Yeah." Shay nodded. "I doubt some alien bitch is gonna figure out a way to force-feed an ancient Atlantean lance magical energy. The only thing is, now we can't move on her quickly. I wanted to finish this shit and not have it hanging over our heads."

James shrugged and slipped under the covers. "If she's running, I'm not worried. When she comes at me, we can try to talk to her and tell her about all this Vax shit and how I'm not gonna call any Vanguard assholes. If she doesn't believe me, then we'll do what we have to do. Not gonna worry about it now. Probably not gonna see her ass for a year, since she bothered to fake her own death."

"Other than Heather and Peyton, no one else knows about this Vax stuff, right?" Shay rolled on her side. "If the government assholes realized you are an alien it'd be bad enough, but if they realize you're an alien supersoldier, they're gonna lock you up in a dungeon and probe your ass for the next twenty years. I don't want to have to kill everyone in the government to rescue you. It'll be annoying and tedious."

James grunted. "Nobody else knows, but we'll have to tell Alison eventually."

"I know, but she's settling into school so well. It won't hurt for her to live a few years without knowing about this shit. By then we'll have taken care of all the loose ends anyway." Shay sighed. "You know how she is. She'll become obsessed with trying to protect you. Insist you use the wish or something."

"Yeah. It can wait." James smiled, warmth all over his face.

Shay blinked. "You're smiling about this?"

"Yeah. It's been a good couple of weeks. Kicked a lot of ass, worked on a new sauce, helped you take down that piece of shit Durand, took out the Eyes, and I… Uh." James chuckled. "What? You want me to bitch? I feel pretty good." He shrugged.

"No." Shay rested on her elbow. "Look, I've tried to leave you alone to work out your shit, but I'm surprised you're not more freaked about this Vax thing or finding out more about your parents."

James shrugged. "They did what they had to to help me, just like Father Thomas. I'm gonna keep doing what I'm doing to make their sacrifices worthwhile. Whispy might bitch, but he's still working for me, so it doesn't matter what he's supposed to be doing or what he cares about. Just because I got a few new memories doesn't change me from before I knew. I'm still James Brownstone, bounty hunter."

Shay smiled softly. "I stand by everything I said. I'll fuck up anyone who comes at you, whatever their reason and whatever planet they're from."

"Nah, it'll be okay. After all, North was so scared of me she faked her own death." James laid his head on the pillow and grunted. "I'm just gonna move on with my life unless Peyton or Heather find something special. Besides, I've got more important shit to worry about."

"More important than someone who wants to kill you?"

James nodded. "Yeah, my future with you. I'm starting to get an idea about something fucking epic."

Shay's brow lifted. "Really?"

"The Cambodia job gave me some ideas."

She laughed. "A monster- and mercenary-infested tomb raid in the jungles of Cambodia gave you an idea about *that*?"

James nodded.

"Sometimes, James, you're even weirder than usual." Shay winked and smiled at him from her pillow. "But I look forward to seeing what you come up with."

Aiyn sighed as she stared out the window of her new home. The high condo provided a view of the sprawling city of Los Angeles. Some might find it pleasing, but staring at glass and concrete didn't bring her any joy. The city lacked the elegance and beauty of her birth city.

Not that it mattered. That was gone, reduced to dust by the Vax.

The gorgeous view of the ocean from her old mansion had soothed her, but that mansion had belonged to her human identity of Erin North—an identity she'd been forced to discard for nothing.

She inhaled deeply. Of all the miscalculations, she'd never expected Shay might use the lance.

"Of course," Aiyn muttered. "After I gave her the big speech about the danger it posed to the world and Durand potentially handing it over to the government, she would think nothing of it. I all but ordered her to use it."

Aiyn's hands curled into fists. Shay's and Brownstone's cyberhounds had been sniffing too hard and too fast. She'd considered killing them, but she had no evidence they understood Brownstone's true nature, or even that Shay Carson herself did.

Some lines couldn't be crossed. Not yet. Not until she had no choice.

All wasn't lost. The foundation would continue under capable leadership, and Aiyn could refocus on being a Shepherd.

I'd let myself become too human; too embroiled in the conflicts on this planet. It's not my duty to solve their wars. It's my duty to protect them from advanced races that might prey on them.

In that sense, discovering the Forerunner was a twisted blessing. Whatever motivated Brownstone's current behavior, his moves so far suggested he was more interested in finishing off Aiyn before he initiated the invasion.

Patience would be the key. Now that her previous human identity was officially dead, the Vax wouldn't be able to track her. She could train, prepare, and experiment.

The nanoform lacked her intelligence. Even with the slowed regeneration of her nanite supply, in a matter of months, she'd have enough nanites to go after James Brownstone directly. Once the Alliance realized what she'd done, they'd punish her anyway, so there was no reason not to try an act of desperation and use the power of the nanites to augment herself.

If I die, I die, but at least I'll die trying to defend this planet.

Aiyn placed her hand against the glass, staring out at the orange-red sky as the sun set over Los Angeles. "No more schemes, Brownstone. No more games. You might be a monster, but you're not a demon or a god.

"I *will* kill you."

AUTHOR NOTES - MICHAEL ANDERLE
DECEMBER 4, 2018

THANK YOU for not only reading this story but these *Author Notes* as well.

(I think I've been good with always opening with "thank you." If not, I need to edit the other *Author Notes*!)

RANDOM (*sometimes*) THOUGHTS?

One Epic Ring.

So, it was that last fight there at the end which named this story. James needed to fetch a ring, and his woman wanted epic.

Like James, I'm pretty straightforward. Thankfully, unlike Shay, my wife didn't leave me to my own devices when picking out the engagement ring.

I might never have asked her to marry me because I couldn't get past that part. I'm serious here.

How did she handle it? She took me to the store, right up to the counter, pointed at the appropriate ring and told me the size she wanted. (*Editor's note: Thumbs-up, Judith! I want to be you when I grow up.*)

AUTHOR NOTES - MICHAEL ANDERLE

Come to think of it, I'm not sure how decided I was asking her to marry me at that time. She was blasting *Single Ladies* (Put a Ring on It) by Beyoncé so much, you would have thought she was paying the radio stations at the time to play it merely to mess with my subconscious.

The other song she seemed to play a lot (Also by Beyoncé) was *Irreplaceable* (To the Left). Between those two songs, it's no wonder I asked in such a short amount of time.

We have been married over eight years now, and I think I've just figured out how damned smart she was at the time.

I'm so screwed.

HOW TO MARKET FOR BOOKS YOU LOVE

We are able to support our efforts with you reading our books, and we appreciate you doing this!

If you enjoyed this or ANY book by any author, especially Indie-published, we always appreciate if you make the time to review a book, since it lets other readers who might be on the fence to take a chance on it as well.

AROUND THE WORLD IN 80 DAYS

One of the interesting (at least to me) aspects of my life is my ability to work from anywhere and at any time. In the future, I hope to re-read my own *Author Notes* and remember my life as a diary entry.

Sitting in Five50 at the Aria Hotel

I just wrote the author notes for *The Dark Mage* about completely fucking evil and what it means. This time I won't go into anything so deep. I think I'll go to the opposite end of the spectrum.

So, what is completely fucking hilarious? Is it a measure of something that makes one person laugh so hard, they lose their fucking mind?

Or is it something that seems to tickle the funny bone of the most people?

If that is true, then I would say that (most likely) physical humor is going to be the universal method of sharing something which is completely fucking hilarious. (*Editor's note: spoken like a male.*)

And if so, then it has to be something which crosses gender and age. Crosses nationalities and race.

Without giving this more than sixty seconds of thought, I'd imagine a funny scene where a guy is kicked in the nuts is something that (can be) completely fucking hilarious.

Except for the person kicked. That person believes the kicker is completely fucking evil.

We would all be right.

And now, I've come back to the dark side, and we are back to evil.

I think I need cookies and milk.

FAN PRICING

If you would like to find out what LMBPN is doing and the books we will be publishing, just sign up at http://lmbpn.com/email/. When you sign up, we notify you of books coming out for the week, any new posts of interest in the books and pop culture arena, and the fan pricing on Saturday.

Ad Aeternitatem,

Michael Anderle

The Daniel Chronicles

The Artifact Enigma (1) - Artifact of the Sky Gods (2) - Artifact Of The True Patriot (3)

The Leira Chronicles

* Martha Carr and Michael Anderle *

Waking Magic (1) - Release of Magic (2) - Protection of Magic (3) - Rule of Magic (4) - Dealing in Magic (5) - Theft of Magic (6) - Enemies of Magic (7) - Guardians of Magic (8)

The Soul Stone Mage Series

* Sarah Noffke and Martha Carr *

House of Enchanted (1) - The Dark Forest (2) - Mountain of Truth (3) - Land of Terran (4) - New Egypt (5) - Lancothy (6) - Virgo (7)

The Kacy Chronicles

* A.L. Knorr and Martha Carr *

Descendant (1) - Ascendant (2) - Combatant (3) - Transcendent (4)

The Midwest Magic Chronicles

* Flint Maxwell and Martha Carr*

The Midwest Witch (1) - The Midwest Wanderer (2) - The Midwest Whisperer (3) - The Midwest War (4)

The Fairhaven Chronicles

* with S.M. Boyce *

Glow (1) - Shimmer (2) - Ember (3) - Nightfall (4)

BOOKS BY MICHAEL ANDERLE

For a complete list of books by Michael Anderle, please visit

www.lmbpn.com/ma-books/

All LMBPN Audiobooks are Available at Audible.com and iTunes. For a complete list of audiobooks visit:

www.lmbpn.com/audible

CONNECT WITH MICHAEL ANDERLE

Michael Anderle Social
   Website:
   http://www.lmbpn.com

Email List:
   http://lmbpn.com/email/

Facebook Here:
   https://www.facebook.com/OriceranUniverse/
   https://www.
facebook.com/TheKurtherianGambitBooks/

www.ingramcontent.com/pod-product-compliance
Lightning Source LLC
Chambersburg PA
CBHW050228110726
47898CB00007B/2060